"Don't worry. I have a plan to lose him."

Grayson wasted no time gunning the engine and creating as much of a dust screen as he possibly could. The van finally fell back a ways to improve visibility.

"Mind if I ask about your plan?" Lauren hadn't relaxed much, although, thankfully, her singing had finally lulled Lily back to sleep.

"I'm trying to get back into town and to the police department. He won't dare try to take the baby with that many law enforcement personnel around." He slowed as little as possible to make the next turn, but their tail was drawing close again.

"What happens after that? Will he leave?" She sounded a little breathless.

"Probably not. We'll figure it out." He tried to sound confident, but wasn't fully convinced himself.

The van was closing in. He tried to floor it, but was too late. The van rammed into the back of the SUV. Hard. Jolting them both forward.

Lily's cries erupted into the confines of the SUV once more.

Sommer Smith teaches high school English and loves animals. She loves reading romances and writing about fairy tales. She started writing her first novel when she was thirteen and has wanted to write romances since. Her three children provide her inspiration to write with their many antics. With two dogs and a horse to keep her active in between, Sommer stays busy traveling to ball games and colleges in two states.

Books by Sommer Smith

Love Inspired Suspense

Under Suspicion
Attempted Abduction

Visit the Author Profile page at Harlequin.com.

ATTEMPTED ABDUCTION

SOMMER SMITH

LOVE INSPIRED SUSPENSE
INSPIRATIONAL ROMANCE

LOVE INSPIRED® SUSPENSE
INSPIRATIONAL ROMANCE

ISBN-13: 978-1-335-72261-4

Attempted Abduction

Recycling programs
for this product may
not exist in your area.

This edition published by arrangement with Harlequin Books S.A.

For questions and comments about the quality of this book, please contact us
at CustomerService@Harlequin.com.

Love Inspired
22 Adelaide St. West, 40th Floor
Toronto, Ontario M5H 4E3, Canada
www.Harlequin.com

Printed in U.S.A.

And the Lord shall deliver me from every evil work,
and will preserve me unto his heavenly kingdom:
to whom be the glory for ever and ever. Amen.
—2 Timothy 4:18

This book is dedicated to my three children, Kate, Gracie and Creighton. The character and grace you each show in your lives is a continual inspiration to me. I thank the Lord every day for blessing me with each of you.

ONE

The NICU was unusually still tonight, with only two babies in the unit. All the other on-call nurses had either been sent home or gone on break.

It was too quiet.

Lauren Beck sat alone beside the newest arrival; a delicate baby girl tagged with the last name Reid. The baby had come five weeks early but already was proving to be a fighter by defying all the odds. The pediatrician on call, Dr. Covington, had declared Baby Girl Reid would likely be allowed to go home in a day or two, barring any complications before then. She had declared her remarkably healthy for a preemie. Lauren had heard her mother refer to her as Lily earlier that day, and the name seemed to fit the tiny infant. Delicate and beautiful.

Turning away from the sleeping babies, Lauren was about to settle in at the computer to update some charts when unease rippled through her. She looked over her shoulder; the practically empty

NICU remained unchanged. Nothing stirred. Everything looked normal. But her nerves prickled. If her instincts were to be trusted, something wasn't right.

The room remained silent except for the buzzing fluorescent lights illuminating the dark night. She resumed her work, hoping it would help to dismiss her nerves.

Earlier in the evening, another nurse had reported a strange phone call requesting information about one of the infants. It went against hospital policy to disclose information to anyone without prior authorization. The caller had become angry, threatening when the nurse had refused to answer his questions. At the time, Dr. Covington had told the nurses to be on their guard, yet she had felt secure enough to leave Lauren alone in the NICU. She must have thought the threat was minimal.

A tiny noise at the entrance to the NICU drew Lauren's attention, and a shadow appeared at the door. She rose from her chair to investigate.

The NICU stayed securely locked at all times, but something made Lauren shiver, even though she knew she should be safe. She had the unsettling feeling she was being watched.

She was being silly. Only authorized hospital personnel had access keycards. No one else could enter without her allowing them in. Still, she moved cautiously toward the door to get a better look.

Reassuring herself that she was perfectly capable of taking care of herself and two babies, Lauren took a deep breath. The earlier phone call was likely just a coincidence. She was being ridiculous. The full moon shining through the hospital window and the quiet of the night were probably just making her jumpy.

She glanced in the direction of the two babies as she strode to the door. It was an odd time—so late at night—to be visiting the NICU, and she had to wonder at the reasons. These babies were her charges right now. Maybe not her children, but it was her responsibility to protect them. She took the responsibility seriously.

The hulking shape of a man filled the glass beside the door. He was scowling at her. His beanie sat low across his forehead and his jacket collar was raised. He wore no identifying hospital pass. *Criminal* was her first thought. She chastised herself for her snap judgment over his appearance and approached the portal.

"May I help you?" she asked through the speaker next to the wall, not daring to open the door. Her voice came out strong and steady, even though her heart was racing.

"I just wanna see my kid." He pointed to Baby Girl Reid. Odd, considering the mother, who had arrived alone, had declared the father to be un-known on the paperwork.

Lauren couldn't—and didn't dare—tell him she knew that. If he was truly the father, he would have to prove it.

If she conceded he could be the father, it made it seem more plausible. But at the moment he had no proof.

"I'm sorry, but I can't let you in without a pass. If you're a parent, you should have gotten one when you and the mother checked in." She placed her hands on her hips, defying her fear by daring him to argue further.

"I didn't come with the mother. I just got here." His face was reddening beneath his beanie.

Angry. *Great.* Not what she needed from this beast of a man. She reminded herself she was per-fectly safe behind the locked door, no matter how intimidating he looked.

"I'm sorry, but you'll have to check with the mother. She can give approval and the staff will issue you a pass. You can come back once you have it." Lauren turned to walk away, but there was a sharp smack against the double-paned glass. She jumped as her heart picked up the pace even more.

Deep breaths. She could handle this.

"Open the door!"

Turning, she saw the man rear back to strike

again. The shatterproof pane vibrated violently when his heavily ringed fist connected with it. Her adrenaline throbbed in tempo with the jarred glass as he pulled a handgun from the waistband of his pants. How had he gotten past security with that?

Lauren wasted no time in running for the emergency alarm. The man was shouting at her as she pushed the button, an angry string of threats and curses following her across the room. He didn't fire the gun, but its mere presence heightened her adrenaline. She knew the glass was also bulletproof, but she didn't want to test it.

When the alarm began to sound, he fled, knocking over a laundry cart in the corridor on his way. He ignored it and kept running. By the time security arrived, he was long gone.

"Lauren, what on earth?" Dr. Covington burst through the door on the heels of security, expression anxious.

"A man just tried to break into the NICU." As she explained what had just happened, Dr. Covington's face paled.

"Thomas, get the mother down here immediately, please." Dr. Covington directed the security guard to Ms. Reid's room.

"Lauren, do you think you could identify the man if you saw him again?" Dr. Covington was on the phone, presumably calling the police.

"Yes, I believe so. Do you think the baby is in

danger?" Lauren's heart was still pounding, but concern for the baby overtook her.

The pediatrician didn't have a chance to answer before the security guard returned, his expression grim.

"Dr. Covington, you said Ms. Reid, room 1204?"

The pediatrician looked up at Thomas with a concerned nod.

"Well, she's gone." Thomas crossed his arms over his broad chest.

"What? She can't be. She hasn't been discharged." Dr. Covington checked a nearby computer monitor to be sure, short nails clicking against the keyboard. "Her OB is Dr. Worman. She hasn't been released."

Thomas shrugged and looked around the NICU once again. "Doesn't look like she went willingly. It's a mess. I'll secure the room, but you'd best get hold of the police."

"She should have had a protector in the room, a bodyguard. He arrived with her and said he would remain with her as long as she was here. Did you see him?" the pediatrician asked in a low voice.

Thomas just shook his head. "No sign of anyone."

Dr. Covington returned to the phone.

Lauren watched in openmouthed horror when she spoke.

"I need to report a possible kidnapping and an attempted break-in to the NICU at Grace Memorial Hospital..." Dr. Covington said. "Mmm-hmm... No, I have a missing patient... Yes, the mother of a newborn in the NICU... Yes, I believe the two incidents to be related."

When Dr. Covington finished with the call, Lauren approached. "What do I need to do?"

"Authorities are on their way. Don't let anyone through that door unless you know them. I don't care what kind of credentials they have." The pediatrician approached the baby, checked her vitals and assured herself that everything was properly attached.

"Was that man really the baby's father?" Lauren looked back toward the door as if expecting the man to return.

"I don't know. Either way, he didn't have clearance to see the baby. You did the right thing, Lauren." Dr. Covington laid a dainty hand on Lauren's shoulder. "The police will probably want to talk to you. I'll have Vanessa paged back to the NICU. Her break was almost over anyway."

Dr. Covington had little more than walked out when Thomas appeared at the door again, this time with a new stranger in tow. Lauren hurried over but stopped short when she got a good look at the man. He was broad-shouldered and tall. His blue eyes took in the NICU with a sweeping glance, seemingly unimpressed with what he saw. His sandy hair, contrary to the other things she noticed about him, was a little messy, and he wore a gray T-shirt that stretched closely over his muscled form. His blue jeans were slightly loose on his slim hips, and there was a gun in a black holster at his waist.

"I'm sorry, but I can't let you in." She spoke before she could think better of it. She almost wished she hadn't when his daunting gaze fixed on her face. "Dr. Covington's orders."

He pulled out a badge, lips pressed in a thin line. "Grayson Thorpe, US marshal. I'm here about the Reid child."

Thomas gave her a nod to indicate it was okay.

"Oh, sorry." Lauren unlocked the door and backed out of the way. "Well, that was fast."

"Pardon?" His expression didn't change much, but his tone hinted that he had no idea what she meant.

"Well, Dr. Covington just reported the incident a few minutes ago. I didn't expect anyone to be here so soon." Her forehead wrinkled between her brows.

"What incident is that?" He placed a hand on one hip. His head angled to one side just a bit. A slight curve to his lips indicated he might be a little amused by her scattered pronouncements.

"He isn't here on behalf of the local police,"

Thomas interjected. "He has other jurisdiction. I haven't filled him in on what happened just yet. I thought it'd be better coming from you."

As Thomas stepped back, Lauren was stricken with undue panic at the thought that he might leave her alone with this man. Other jurisdiction? What was that supposed to mean? She was out of her element here.

"Thomas, wait. You're the one who discovered the mother missing. You should stay." Lauren fought to keep her calm voice from warbling a bit. The security guard's presence reassured her. It was familiar. Not like this man before her now.

"I don't care who tells me what happened, but somebody better do it soon." A thunderous expression was taking over Marshal Thorpe's face and Lauren winced. Now she really didn't want to talk. She didn't like it when people tried to intimidate her.

She relented, however, since the baby's safety was at stake. "A man tried to get into the NICU without any credentials. He claimed to be Baby Girl Reid's father. When I wouldn't allow him entrance, he got angry." Lauren paused, eyeing the baby, who was beginning to awaken with little grunts.

"So he left?" The marshal raised an eyebrow.

"More like fled when I sounded the alarm." She moved toward the fussing baby.

He took out his phone and started typing something into it. "You didn't recognize the man?" His piercing blue eyes fixed on her face as he looked up at her. He seemed to be watching for any sort of sign that might give away answers.

Lauren felt too exposed, though she had done nothing wrong. She was having trouble focusing. The questions, the attempted break-in—it was all becoming too much.

"I'm here to pick her up. I need to know who tried to take the child. Did you recognize the man?" The marshal's voice held an impatient edge.

Thomas had slipped away while Lauren had been distracted with the marshal. She realized he was absent a little too late—she wanted to flee along with him.

Baby Girl Reid had set up a good howl now, but Lauren paused to consider the marshal's latest question. Her face drawn, she shook her head before turning back to the child. "No, I'm pretty sure I had never seen him before."

"And the mother is missing?" Marshal Thorpe's brow furrowed.

Lauren nodded. "The security guard said it looked like there had been a scuffle."

He pressed his lips tightly closed. "There should have been another marshal protecting the mother. She's the daughter of a senator, and he keeps security with her at all times."

Thomas strode in just in time to hear the comment. "We found him—just now, actually. An orderly heard something coming from a supply closet. There was a man bound and gagged inside. He was kicking and screaming when they pulled him out."

Lauren's eyes widened, but she took the opportunity to pick up the baby girl. The infant calmed immediately but squirmed and rooted as Lauren cradled her to her chest. "Is the baby in serious danger?"

By the time she looked at Marshal Thorpe's face, he was sporting a fierce scowl. "It would seem so. The baby's mother is the daughter of Senator Jack Jamison Reid. He has a lot of enemies. I was hired to protect her."

Lauren felt the blood drain from her face. She had never experienced such a situation before. "Powerful enemies?"

"It's likely the baby, the mother and now you are all in a great deal of danger." He glanced at the door. "He'll be back. We need to get her out of here, ASAP."

Lauren was shaking her head. "What does this guy want with a baby?"

"I'm sorry—I don't have time for all this right now," the marshal asserted. "Besides, we don't have enough information just yet to know. But Jack Jamison Reid was a lawyer before becoming a senator and has never been known to go easy on anyone. He keeps an extensive security detail in place for not only himself but also his daughter at all times. He seems to expect some threats."

"Then why wouldn't they have just hired someone to protect the baby? Why wasn't someone here to protect her before this happened?" Lauren blinked at him a moment before realization set in. "Because she came early, right? They weren't prepared."

"Didn't help that she was born in the middle of the night, either." Marshal Thorpe looked almost angry about it. He rested one hand on his chest in an unconscious gesture.

"I don't think that was anyone's choice." Lauren snapped the words, annoyed with his gruff attitude.

Before he could respond, Dr. Covington returned. She looked ready to do battle as she challenged the marshal. "Thomas said you are trying to take the baby."

So that was where Thomas had gone, Lauren realized.

"It's the only way to keep her safe." He braced his fists at his waist, as if ready to fire back.

Lauren spoke up. "She is premature. She really should stay in the NICU for another day or two."

Dr. Covington looked at Baby Girl Reid, nestled in Lauren's arms and sucking rhythmically on a bottle that Lauren had just pulled from a nearby bottle warmer. "She's right. The baby needs to stay here."

The marshal was already shaking his head. "You're putting the whole hospital and everyone in it in serious danger if she does."

"What do you mean?" Lauren was unconvinced.

"If my sources are correct, the baby could be the child of Arnold Romine, DC's infamous drug kingpin. If that turns out to be true, Senator Reid is right to have extra protection for his grandchild. That would just put her in that much more danger. And from what you just told me, it sounds like she's definitely in danger."

Grayson looked at the small bundle in the arms of the pretty young nurse. Who knew such a tiny thing could cause such massive problems? And be so terrifying…

The pediatrician who seemed to be in charge was frowning in thought. She seemed to grasp the truth of what he'd said but, if he had to guess, was battling the professionalism so deeply ingrained in her. "It could mean you're risking her life," she finally said.

"How sick is she? If she is well enough to travel, not moving her could risk dozens of other lives…" He knew it sounded cold, but this was a tough situation. He had to make her understand. It was his job.

The young nurse challenged him again. "How can you ask her to value one life over another?"

He kept his eyes fixed on the doctor. "I'm not trying to risk any lives here. I will do everything I can to keep her safe and healthy. That means keeping her under constant medical supervision if possible. I just can't leave her here."

He glanced again at the nurse, thinking she might start to concede. Instead, her green eyes snapped with fire. He felt a spark of admiration for her.

"So you want to just pick up and leave with a tiny, helpless life whom we should all be protecting. How are you going to keep her safe?" she asked, her stance defiant despite her arms being full. "Don't you think she needs medical care until we know she is strong enough to travel?"

"That's my intent, other than the fact that we have to travel. There's no choice. The risk is greater if we don't move her. But I aim to protect her." He looked at the baby again. He would rather be in charge of Savannah's safety, but a falling-out with his boss had had him assigned to Baby Girl Reid instead of her mother. There had recently been some false accusations raised against him, but his supervisor had yet to disclose where they'd come from. Despite his inexperience with infants, he knew he had to prove he could do the job.

"Taking her from the NICU could endanger her health. Isn't that important to you?" The nurse's voice had softened a bit, probably hoping to appeal to his emotional side. She didn't know he had been forced to block that off, thanks to his job. Maybe even years before that, if he were honest.

But this wasn't about his family history. "Is she so critical? Do you have any reason to believe she will be in danger without medical intervention?" He turned his attention back to the doctor to ask the question.

Dr. Covington thought for a moment. "No, she isn't critical. But it's hospital protocol to hold a premature infant for observation."

"So she could survive without the hospital monitors and equipment?" Grayson ignored the feel of the nurse's indignant stare on his face.

Dr. Covington considered this before nodding. "I'll let you take her to a safe house under one condition."

Grayson heard the nurse suck in a breath, but he remained focused on the doctor. "What's that?"

Dr. Covington gave the nurse a look he could only define as apologetic. "Lauren goes with you. She's the best pediatric nurse we have in the NICU. If anything goes wrong with Baby Girl Reid's health, she'll know what to do until you can get her to a hospital."

The nurse's eyes widened. "Dr. Covington, you can't be serious. This baby needs close monitoring."

The doctor nodded. "Which you can take care of. She's showing none of the usual complications seen in a preemie. And this is an emergency situation."

"Get your things." Grayson gestured for the nurse to gather whatever she needed. He wanted to sigh when she just stood there gaping at him, the baby quietly working the bottle in Lauren's arms.

"Who says I agree?" She looked like a mad hen, only a lot cuter.

He ignored the thought. "I don't have time for this."

Dr. Covington began unhooking the monitors while the nurse continued to hold the bottle with one hand and the infant in the other and stare.

Grayson took the baby as soon as she was freed and started for the door.

The nurse shrieked. "What are you doing?"

"I'm taking this baby somewhere safe, with or without you." He didn't slow his pace at all. His instincts told him she would follow. Sometimes the job just had to be done. There was no time to waste.

It was silent behind him for two beats before he

heard tennis shoe soles whispering a quick rhythm behind him.

"Wait!" She laid a hand on his shoulder. "We need some diapers and formula and things to get us by until we can get more."

He looked down at the baby, then gave the nurse a nod.

"Where exactly are we going?" Her voice wavered at his back. He could hear her gathering supplies from a cabinet behind him.

"I haven't received orders on our final destination yet." He heard her suck in a breath. It probably seemed daunting to her, though it was something he had grown accustomed to. "It's likely it will be a pretty long distance."

Dr. Covington called their attention to where she stood watching them, halting them both with her words. "How should I direct the authorities when they arrive and want to question Nurse Beck?"

She gestured at Lauren, and Grayson realized he was about to turn this woman's life upside down and didn't even know her name. He reminded himself it was just the nature of the job. He gave the doctor a piercing look. "Tell them it has been taken under the jurisdiction of the US Marshals Service."

The doctor nodded and looked again at the nurse. "You know how to reach me if you need me. I'll see that your shifts are covered."

Grayson was surprised at the nurse's quiet ac-quiescence as they trekked through the hospi-tal. They made their way to the lot out back and walked toward a big black SUV. He had parked as close to the building as possible to provide enough cover to get the baby inside, knowing it would take precious minutes to secure the infant.

"What about a car seat?" Lauren jumped in front of him, clearly intending to block his path to the vehicle if she didn't like his response.

"Already taken care of." He motioned for her to look inside.

She opened the back door to find a baby carrier already secured on the seat. She gave him a nod of approval. "That's a relief."

"Did you think I just planned to toss the baby in the back seat?" He couldn't keep the irritation from his voice.

"You never know. I don't know anything at all about you." She took the baby from his arms, her hand brushing against the scar beneath his T-shirt. He drew in a sharp breath as she began to settle her into the carrier.

If she noticed his indrawn breath, she didn't mention it.

"Right. Well, you can rest assured, as required by my job, I always play by the rules when it comes to safety. I'm protective. And intelligent."

He practically growled the words at her. "That's about all you need to know right now."

She stopped and gave him a startled look, like it had never occurred to her that she might have insulted him. He wanted to laugh. She was completely unexpected.

"What's so funny?" The veins stood out on her small hands as her slender fingers adjusted the straps around the baby's chest.

"You get ruffled easily for someone who likes to hand out insults." He motioned for her to get in the front passenger seat as he closed the back door. "Come on. We need to get going."

She obeyed, but as soon as they were in the vehicle, she returned fire. "I do not hand out insults. Maybe you're just easily offended."

"What? You just practically accused me of being too dumb to remember a car seat."

"I didn't— Well... I didn't mean to sound that way. It's just something I didn't really expect you to think of. I mean, you don't seem like the type to be a father. My apologies."

His brow furrowed. "How do you know I'm not a father?"

She shrugged. "You seem uncomfortable with the baby."

He couldn't argue with that. He was surprised she had so quickly picked up on it, though. "It's true I haven't spent much time around newborns."

He put the SUV into Drive and checked his mirrors thoroughly before pulling out. He didn't see anything suspicious at the moment, but it was impossible to be too cautious at a time like this.

"In any case, I'd rather you not make assumptions. Just ask me. Lack of communication in a situation like this can get people killed." He knew she would probably think he was overreacting, but there were some things that needed to be established. Lives depended on it. "So, just so we are clear, I'm in charge here. You listen and do what I tell you first, ask questions later."

"Fine." She shot him a look that said it didn't sit well with her but that she would yield for the time being. He liked that she was feisty, though her temperament could put them in danger if she didn't watch it.

"Oh, and by the way." Lauren looked at the baby. "I think the mother named her Lily. So, if that's okay with you, that's what we will call her. She needs a name."

He nodded and checked the mirrors again, still seeing nothing out of the ordinary.

He looked over in time to catch Lauren typing something on her phone. "What are you doing? Why do you have that?"

"What now?" She threw up her hands.

"Your phone. It's traceable. Anyone who wants to know your whereabouts can track you. If whoever is after her discovers you have left the hospital with Lily, it would be easy to figure out where to look for you." He held out his hand.

She clutched her phone to her chest, giving him an offended look. "Not unless they know my number. I'm not in the habit of giving it out to just anyone."

He frowned and shook his head at her. "Pretty much anyone with a background in crime will be able to get it. I'm sure the hospital has it, right?"

"Yes, but that information is private." Her expression was stricken.

"And any experienced hacker can still retrieve it. What if whoever's trying to get the baby finds out you're with us?" He hated to be the one to shatter her bubble of security, but the phone had to go.

She wasn't giving up easily, though. "What if I turn it off? Or on airplane mode? Isn't there a way to keep it from being tracked?"

"It's risky. Is a cell phone important enough to risk the baby's life—and yours?" He had to hope that appealing to her sense of self-preservation and protective instincts would work.

"I just need to keep in touch with my family. But if you think it's too risky… I understand."

Her dejection was almost comical. What was with her attachment to the device? "I do, actually. If I will allow you to use my phone to check in with your family, would that suffice?"

She gave a small nod. "My sister has a serious medical condition. They might need to reach me at any time, but if I can check in with them frequently, that would help."

"I'm sorry to hear that. You can make calls on my secure phone anytime you need to, though. It will be safer." He gestured for her device.

"What do you plan to do with it?" she asked, holding it out with obvious reluctance.

He instructed her to power off the phone and removed the SIM card, then asked her to place it into the console of the SUV in answer to her question. "Don't turn that phone on for any reason."

She looked completely panic-stricken. "How often can I call to check in? They also might need to get in touch with me from the hospital—"

"You're going to have to go off the grid for a bit. Hopefully, it won't be long and we'll have this whole situation resolved. You can check in as often as you like. Why do you expect your family to need you so frequently? What is wrong with your sister?"

"She has cystic fibrosis and is awaiting a lung for transplant. I help my mother with her care from time to time."

Grayson felt a little remorse in that moment. "I really am sorry. But we can't risk anyone knowing you're with me. It might put them in danger, as well. Safety comes first." He glanced at his mirrors again. "Right now, I'm just trying to make sure we aren't being followed." He sighed, then asked, "Can you give them a good reason to be out of touch for a day or two? At least let them know you will be checking in from a strange number from time to time?"

"Yes. It just worries me to be out of contact." She looked like she might start crying and his gut clenched in response.

He understood her concerns but had no idea how to correct the issue. He knew she wouldn't want to put her family in danger, though. Perhaps he should try to explain that sometimes the bad guys used family members to get what they wanted. That he knew she wouldn't want it to come to that, so it was safer to avoid contact until the situation was resolved.

But then he turned a corner and found the road blocked by a big white van. "Uh-oh. This isn't good."

There were structures on either side of the street, with narrow sidewalks between the road and the buildings. There was no way around the van.

Grayson slammed on the brakes with a shouted warning. He then threw the SUV into Reverse, trying to get going again before the van could follow. But it took the big SUV some time to accelerate, and by the time he sped away, the van was in close pursuit.

The baby began to cry, filling the SUV with her high-pitched little wails.

"Hold on, Miss Beck." He performed some evasive driving maneuvers to try to lose the van.

"I think at a time like this it's safe to use first names, no? Lauren." She was still trying to right herself from being tumbled in place, glad she had secured her seat belt.

Lily was crying in earnest now. "Right. Do me a favor, Lauren, and keep an eye out for that van while I try to lose it. Let me know if the driver tries to start shooting."

"Shooting?" Her high-pitched reply told him she hadn't expected that.

"It's unlikely, since he seems to be alone. And I'm sure he was told no shooting around the baby." Grayson hit the gas.

"Unlikely. But not impossible." She unbuckled and climbed into the back seat with the baby while he drove in a straight line.

"No, not completely. But he likely won't risk hitting the baby. Just stay low as much as you can and still keep watch." He kept his voice even, hoping to encourage calm. They were almost out of town, at least.

To his surprise, Lauren began to sing to the baby in a soft, sweet voice. Lily began to quiet a little and Grayson found he had to focus on what he was doing. She had a beautiful voice.

She paused her singing for a moment. "He's still there but falling back some."

Lauren resumed her lullaby, but Grayson interrupted. "Okay, then. Hold on. I'm going to try to completely lose him."

He began to slow the SUV, but just as they came to an intersection, another car came from out of nowhere and was headed right at them. He slammed hard on the brakes and tried to swerve without losing control of the SUV. It rocked hard and they barely slid by without colliding with the other vehicle. The car just kept going, leading him to believe it was in league with the van.

While Grayson was trying to recover, however, the white van drew closer. Lauren didn't even have to tell him. "Great. There isn't much of anywhere to lose him out here."

"So what now, then?" She had to be loud to be heard over the crying baby.

The infant's wails accelerated the fraying of his nerves. He needed to concentrate, but a crying baby wasn't something he could easily block out.

"I'll have to double back. We can't take any chances on giving up our location." Grayson thought hard, trying to come up with a route that might help him lose their tail. His large hand moved automatically to the scar on his chest, rubbing it with his fingers as if to make the throbbing go away. It was a habit he hardly noticed doing anymore.

The town of Birchfield wasn't small, but once a person got too far out, there weren't a lot of different roads to take. At least they were out of DC. This was usually a fairly quiet area, which was probably why their assailant had waited until they'd made it this far to give chase.

Putting his thoughts aside, he took the first turn-off that came available, hoping it would lead to where he thought it would. The network of roads around a town like Birchfield were pretty predictable, meaning a few blocks down he would find another turn that would eventually lead him in a big square right back to town. No criminal would want to chase them through town, especially not right to city hall and the police station.

"He's getting closer." Lauren sounded a little panicked in the back seat. He wasn't sure she wouldn't start crying right along with Lily. He needed to encourage her.

"Don't worry. I have a plan to lose him." He saw the turnoff he was hoping for in the distance, so he floored it for a few seconds, then made a right. He wasn't yet sure how he would ever be able to leave the police department without someone following them again. He would work it out somehow.

The turn worked to his advantage, Grayson

soon discovered, because it was a dirt road. He wasted no time gunning the engine and creating as much of a dust screen as he possibly could. The driver of the van, also having made the turn, finally fell back a ways to improve his visibility.

Grayson sped to the next turn. It would still be a close call getting into town before their tail realized what he was doing and tried something else.

"Mind if I ask about your plan?" Lauren hadn't relaxed much, although, thankfully, her singing had finally lulled Lily back to sleep.

"I'm trying to get back into town and to the police department. He won't dare try to take the baby with that many law enforcement personnel around. We will just have to pray they aren't all out on patrol or on calls when we get there." He slowed as little as possible to make the next turn, but their tail was drawing close again.

"Oh. Okay, good idea. And what happens after that? Will he leave?" She sounded a little breathless.

"Probably not. We'll figure it out." He tried to sound confident but wasn't fully convinced himself. Sure, they would do something. He just wasn't entirely sure what that something would be.

"Um, Grayson? I think he might be onto your plan."

He turned his attention to his rearview mirror just in time to see what she meant. The van was closing in. He tried to floor it but was too late. The van rammed into the back of the SUV. Hard. Jolting them both forward.

Lily's cries erupted into the confines of the SUV once more.

TWO

Lauren fought the urge to scream right along with the newborn. She knew that Marshal Thorpe—Grayson—was doing everything he could, but the situation was like nothing she had ever experienced. And she had been through a lot.

"Hold on, Lauren." Grayson's full lips pressed together in concentration as he worked to keep control of the huge vehicle. He punched the gas once more and tried to keep ahead of the van. It worked for a little bit, but it wasn't long before the other vehicle advanced on them again, ramming into the rear bumper once more. The SUV fishtailed as Grayson struggled to maintain control.

The back-and-forth continued for far too long, so Lauren prayed for relief. Occasionally, Grayson would glance back at her in concern, but he did a remarkable job of remaining calm and keeping them on the road.

Lauren had just about given up hope that they might lose the van when lights and sirens approached from a distance. The white van shot around the SUV and took off.

Relief filled her when the county patrol car followed the van and they were finally able to slow down and catch their breath. "That was way too close."

Grayson compressed his lips as he glanced at her in the rearview mirror. She wondered what that tight-lipped expression meant. Was he just wondering how long they would be safe? Or did he already regret bringing her along? Lily, having calmed, was on the verge of falling asleep.

"We would have made it to town before he could have done any real damage." Grayson adjusted the vent.

Was he really so self-assured? That had been terrifying. Maybe not so new to him, but still horrible.

Lauren bit back a retort, thinking that it wouldn't help anything. Maybe he was trying to reassure her. She didn't know much about him, but it struck her as self-assurance—maybe a little too much confidence in his abilities. Or maybe she had just experienced too much of the same from men in her past and was assuming that.

She studied what she could see of his profile. Sure, he was handsome. But Lauren knew better than to be fooled by an attractive face. Most men who looked like Grayson Thorpe tended to be quite aware of it and used their good looks to their advantage. Her late husband had been proof of that.

"So, what now? Do we go into town or to the safe house?" She wanted to distract herself from her own thoughts as much as she wanted to know the plan.

"Going into town would only put us at risk of gaining another tail. There's no reason to."

She cringed. She was pretty bad at this—whatever *this* was. Running from bad guys? Hanging out with a US marshal?

"Of course. I just thought you'd need to speak to the local police." She snapped out the words, but he didn't seem to take any notice of her sharp tone. Lauren told herself there was no reason to turn defensive. But she was embarrassed. She was glad he at least couldn't see how red her face was right now.

"Nope. I'll report to the US Marshals Service. They will take care of the rest." He glanced at his mirrors again, but Lauren suspected it was more out of habit than of any real concern. He almost looked bored.

With Lily sleeping, the silence began to stretch into an uncomfortable awkwardness. The fact that she was alone with a stranger began to sink in, and Lauren had to breathe deeply for a moment. The reality of what she had agreed to was overwhelming. She focused on the baby's tiny face, trying to ignore the sensation of panic about to overtake her. This precious baby needed her. Protection from her would-be abductor would mean nothing if she had complications from her premature birth. Grayson might have a big job keeping the bad guys from kidnapping her, but Lauren knew that keeping Lily alive and healthy might be just as difficult if complications arose.

"Everything still okay back there?"

Grayson's voice startled her. "Um. Yeah. We're good."

He watched her for a minute as their eyes held in the rearview mirror. She knew he was only gauging her response, but something was happening to her pulse. *You know better than to react to men like him*, she chastised herself. In her experience, men like Grayson Thorpe—handsome, self-assured and persuasive—always hurt people like her.

"I'm good." She knew she was repeating herself, but she feared he might read her thoughts.

Her conscience pricked at her. She didn't know Grayson well enough to make such assumptions about him. She needed to let go of the past and to stop allowing it to color her views of other people. She breathed a quick prayer for guidance.

"Good." He finally broke the visual hold. "Let me know if you need anything. We have a long drive ahead."

"Where are we going?" She didn't like the sound of this.

"Out of state. Hopefully somewhere the kidnappers won't find us." He glanced at a GPS map on his SUV's display screen.

"Out of state...where?" Lauren wasn't about to settle for such a vague response.

"Somewhere south. I haven't received the exact location yet." He didn't seem in any mood to comply with her demands.

"South. Like Florida? Georgia? Tennessee?" She could only think of a few of those good ol' Southern states at the moment.

"Maybe. Could be anywhere. Arkansas, Oklahoma, Louisiana." His tone said he really didn't feel like explaining himself to her.

Still vague and even more disconcerting. Those states were a long way from Birchfield, DC, and from where her family lived. Her stomach clenched. She had never been far out of DC. It seemed like a whole other world in those unfamiliar states.

Lily needs you. Lily needs you. She chanted the words silently to calm her nerves. She wouldn't let this stranger see how terrified she was of the situation. Her father's words came back to her from so long ago. *Be brave, little one. You'll never know how far you can go until you get there.*

His memory had gotten her through many difficult times, even though she didn't have that many recollections. Almost too young to remember when he died, she did know that he would see her through this situation, as well.

Lauren looked up to find Marshal Thorpe watching her in the mirror again. "Is something wrong?"

The question sounded a bit sharp to her ears, but he only shrugged. "Nah. Just wondering how much trouble you're going to be."

Her face reddened in anger. "How much—? You, Marshal Thorpe, are a rude man!"

To her consternation, he laughed. "I thought we already agreed to first names, Lauren."

She huffed. "Whatever."

He was wearing a cocky grin, but at least he was focused on the road again and not her reflection in the rearview mirror. She didn't dare contemplate why his scrutiny made her squirm.

"Are you, though?" He looked up at her once again.

"Am I what?" She didn't have a clue what he was asking.

"Are you going to be a lot of trouble?" The cocky grin was back.

She just scowled at him. Was he teasing her? She had no idea how to respond to his questions.

"No, really. I need to know what to be prepared for here."

Lauren straightened her shoulders. "I have never been a moment's trouble to anyone a day in my life. I take care of myself."

"Good." His grin slid away. "Then we should get along just fine."

Grayson knew he probably wasn't coming off as the most charming man to Lauren. He wanted to tease her and to see her smile, and he was allowing that, somewhat, though he knew he enjoyed her response to his teasing a little more than he should. He had to keep some distance between them, despite his personal wishes. The more he thought about it, the more he regretted having to bring her along. The truth was, though, he hadn't really had a choice. The baby needed protection, and she also needed constant care—all the better if it were given by a trained medical professional. He was far from qualified to provide both. The first wasn't a big deal, but the latter... He didn't have the first inkling of how to take care of a newborn baby—and definitely not a premature one.

It bothered him, though, how pale and nervous Lauren looked. He didn't doubt for an instant that this situation was new to her. It couldn't be easy, either. He just didn't have any idea how to help her with any of it.

So he responded the only way he knew how. And she probably thought he was a self-assured jerk.

It wasn't that he disliked her or didn't care about her feelings. The truth was, he didn't have a lot of patience for drama, and he was especially leery of giving someone his trust. He hoped she would prove to be trustworthy, because he didn't know if he was ready to deal with a situation like Rebecca's again.

True, Lauren was probably stronger than she looked. But you never knew how well you could trust someone until they were put in a situation that required it.

Looking at her reflection now, though, he wasn't sure why he felt so off-kilter. Something about her made his confidence waver. It wasn't about trust, really. He knew he could do his job whether he could trust her or not, but for some reason, she brought out a desire to prove himself. The funny thing for Grayson was that no matter how rattled she might look, she somehow still seemed to be in complete control while his emotions were in a flux. The woman was an enigma.

Growing up with nothing but brothers had taught Grayson to respond with witty remarks and competition to establish pecking order. But he had no need to compete with Lauren and she wasn't responding well to his witty remarks.

And that brought him right back to the question of how to deal with Lauren Beck.

"Do you need anything?" He couldn't think of another way to find out.

Lauren shook her head. "Just keep driving while the baby's sleeping. She'll be demanding things soon enough."

It occurred to him that although he had remembered the car seat, he was unprepared for the rest of the child's needs. He had picked up a package of preemie diapers before going to the hospital, but the huge selection of formula and bottles had left him baffled. He hoped Lauren could help him out on that score. As for anything else, he didn't have a clue what a baby would need.

Lauren seemed to know what he was thinking. "I have a couple of bottles of formula that I brought from the hospital, but she will need more soon. If we could get her a couple of little sleepers, a blanket or two and some diapers, along with the formula, we should make it okay for a couple of days. If it's longer, the list will grow, I'm afraid."

That didn't sound too promising. "Grow? Like how? What else could something that tiny need?"

Lauren laughed. "You'd be surprised. But we will worry about that when—if—the time comes."

His gut clenched. He hadn't really considered

what all would be involved in this assignment. The thought of spending a prolonged period of time with an attractive woman and a baby scared him more than facing down Arnold Romine and his whole gang.

He would just have to see to it that that didn't happen.

If all went well, they would catch the kidnapper by this time tomorrow and Lily would be reunited with her mother. At least, he hoped he could find her by then. If she had been kidnapped, that would be a whole other problem.

He only wanted to go back to his happy, solitary bachelor life. Wouldn't his brothers have fun with this assignment the next time he went home? Of course, he would tolerate it, because most of the time he was helping do the same for one of his brothers. It was just something they did.

Lauren had stilled and quieted. He couldn't help but notice that it was taking her a little longer than usual to blink. "You should get some rest while the baby is asleep. We are likely in for at least a day or two of driving."

She took in the cloudy morning outside the window, not even blinking at his pronouncement. "I'm used to being awake at odd hours. I usually work second or third shift in the NICU. And I usually work twelve-hour shifts."

"And how many hours has it been since you

went in?" He couldn't look at her now, but he still felt the weight of his own question between them. He sensed her checking the time on her watch, saw the rotation of her wrist out of the corner of his eye.

"About fourteen hours, I guess." She sounded weary, though he didn't doubt she meant it to be nonchalance.

He glanced at the dash clock. "Hmm. More time has passed than I thought."

She didn't respond, only stared through the window. Was she trying to think of a way out of this? If so, that would make two of them.

"You really should sleep. I can promise you right now I'll be worse than useless at taking care of a baby." He wasn't even going to waste time being embarrassed about it. She might as well know now. She would figure it out soon enough anyway.

"It can't be that bad. Haven't you ever been around a baby before?" Her voice held a hint of laughter.

He ignored it. "Nope."

"Not even a little? Like, no nieces, nephews, cousins, anything?" Now she sounded a little shocked.

"I've always kept my distance from any newborns that came along." He was sounding like a jerk again. But it was true. Mainly because he was half-scared of newborns. Or any child under the age of twelve, for that matter.

She was quiet for a moment. "They don't bite, you know. They don't even have any teeth."

The chuckle escaped before he could stop it. She saw through him far too easily, but her stoically delivered comment hit him right in the funny bone.

"I guess you would know." He laughed again, glancing in the mirror to see that her expression had eased, and she could possibly be fighting a grin.

"I won't leave you alone with her until we are both confident you can handle her."

"Sounds like a deal. But you can sleep while she sleeps." He let one side of his mouth relax, hoping a silly, crooked grin would put her at ease.

Her smile faded in the mirror. "Grayson?"

Uh-oh. He didn't like her tone. "What?"

"How had you planned to take care of the baby if you hadn't brought me along?" One eyebrow quirked slightly.

He looked away, not sure how to explain things to her. "I was supposed to have a colleague meet me when I left the hospital. I wasn't sure I would be taking the baby with me right away, but when someone tried to kidnap her, it seemed the only logical solution. I didn't want to risk the safety of more of the hospital staff."

"So why me? Wouldn't you rather have chosen an older, more experienced nurse? Maybe someone who could handle this situation better?" Her voice warbled a bit on the admission. She didn't like the weakness but knew it was there.

He wanted to reassure her that she was more than capable.

"I wouldn't say I chose, exactly. If you recall, that was your doctor friend. But I would have chosen you, regardless, to be honest."

She fought a pleased grin. "Why is that?"

"You looked ready to do battle over that tiny baby. I needed a partner in this situation. Someone who would help me protect this child. I can't imagine anyone better for the task."

Lauren was a little shaken by this man and his crooked grin. He was easier not to like when he was wearing a growl. Liking him was something she hoped to avoid, considering she wasn't ready for another relationship. But Grayson Thorpe was more likable than she'd first thought, and the compliment he had just thrown her way was not one she took lightly. It kind of softened her insides a little more where he was concerned. No, that wasn't exactly true. His sweet words had almost turned her to mush.

So now she was curious about what the original plan had been, before the kidnapper had come along.

Now wasn't the time to press for details, though, so she decided to take his advice and try to sleep. *Try* was about all she could do. Her eyelids might have been heavy, but her mind was going full-out with at least a thousand thoughts per minute. Like, how long would it take to catch Romine? What should she tell her family? How much would her normal life be disrupted by this? And how was this imposed duty going to affect her job at the hospital?

Lauren had been seeking a promotion to a better shift, so she hoped that her cooperation would find her in a favorable light with her supervisor. She hadn't been working in the NICU for long, but she truly loved her job. Keeping it was most important. Lauren had an ill sibling to help her mother care for, and any raise in pay, no matter how slight, would make a difference.

But Britlan would want Lauren to take care of Lily. In fact, her little sister was so fond of babies that she had declared a desire to follow in Lauren's footsteps. Of course, Lauren knew it would have much to do with how healthy the fourteen-year-old remained, and that depended entirely on them getting her adequate treatment. Britlan's rapidly worsening cystic fibrosis meant she would need a transplant soon, though a new lung had not yet been located. She was on the waiting list, but for Britlan to stay on it meant Lauren needed to make enough money to keep her sister in good medical care. She had to be healthy enough for the transplant and Lauren had to remain employed to afford the cost of the procedure. Her mother certainly couldn't handle it on her own.

Lauren would have to do everything she could to make sure she wasn't stuck with Grayson any longer than necessary. She needed to be back home. She often took care of Britlan so that her mother, who hated to leave Britlan alone for even a few hours, could take care of a few errands.

The problem was that Lauren had no idea how to get things with the marshal moving forward at a faster pace.

She supposed she could start by getting some information. She swallowed the nervous lump that arose in her throat when she began to consider what questions to ask. She might as well start with the one burning her mind. Did he need her assistance indefinitely or did he have other plans in place? And how long did he expect this to take?

She cleared her throat.

Lily wailed.

Lauren leaned in close to see what was wrong. "Uh-oh."

Grayson pulled the wheel slightly as he looked

in the rearview mirror. "What do you mean 'uh-oh'? What's wrong?"

"We are going to have to stop for a dry change of clothes. I think her diaper has leaked all over the gown she has on." Lauren wrinkled her nose, feeling the pull of her lips into a grimace.

"Oh, great. You didn't bring a change of clothes from the hospital?" He practically rolled his eyes.

"You didn't give me time." She frowned at his reflection.

"Can't you just strip her down? Wrap her in a blanket or something?" He shook his head at her.

"She's a newborn. Preemie or not, she isn't used to exposure. It isn't healthy for her, and she won't be happy. Do you want to listen to her squall for the next fifty miles?"

He had the decency to look contrite. "I see what you mean."

She'd noticed he didn't exactly say she was right.

"I'll pull off onto the next exit. I think we are near Roanoke. I can stop there if it's not too far."

By the time they took an exit large enough to lead them to a place with shopping venues, Lily was having a full-on angry fit. Grayson looked like he wanted to cover his ears. "Good grief. That baby has some powerful lungs."

Lauren nodded. "That's a good thing. Do you want to shop or to stay with Lily? I'd rather not take her into a store wailing like this. And I also hate to take her in undressed or in wet clothing."

He looked like she had just dropped the most earth-shattering news he had ever heard on him. "I don't shop. I mean, I don't know how to shop for a newborn. And I can't leave her."

"Okay, then stay with Lily and I will go." She had finished stripping the wet clothes off the baby and changing her diaper. Wrapping her tightly in a dry blanket, she held Lily out to Grayson and watched his blue eyes go wide.

"You promised you wouldn't leave me alone with her. And she's mad." He looked utterly petrified.

She wanted to laugh. "Well, it would only be for a few minutes. But that's okay. I'm sure you can pick up a couple of sleepers and gowns without any trouble. Just get the Enfamil Low Iron and a couple of bottles made for newborns. I think about four will do while we are traveling, but we will have to come up with a way to sterilize them. Maybe they will have a portable sterilizer in stock."

Lauren stopped talking when he started to shake his head. "I don't know what you are talking about. I have no idea what's worse—a screaming baby or a newborn shopping list. Is there no other way?"

She thought for a moment. "I can see if we have a dry blanket. If we wrap her tightly and keep her in the carrier, she should be okay for a few minutes. As soon as we get something, we can dress her."

He was looking at the baby like she was an alien, though her cries had softened somewhat now that the wet clothes had been removed.

"Or I could just go and take her with me." She said it softly, and his eyes grew large. It was obvious he didn't want to let either of them out of his sight.

"No, we'll all go." His face was a resigned mask. "See if you can find us directions to the nearest store with infant supplies."

Lauren wanted to ask how he was blocking the GPS signal on his own phone when he handed it to her to do the search, but she bit back her question. She supposed marshals had to have a way around those sorts of things. Now they had to concentrate on Lily.

Once she located a store and they pulled into the parking lot, Grayson told her to stay put. "Let me do a sweep of the area before you take the baby out."

She waited as he scanned the area, located all security cameras and assured himself all was clear. He motioned to her and she began to detach the baby carrier from the base. He was there to take the screaming infant, carrier and all, while she led the way. She noticed an older couple watching them with a sweet smile. No doubt they thought them a happy couple with a newborn. Little did they know of the convoluted situation.

Inside the store, Lauren wasted no time in locating everything they needed. Once the purchases were made, she asked where he wanted her to change the baby.

He looked at her like she had lost her mind. "In the SUV. We can't take a risk on staying here too long."

Lauren nodded, and they made their way toward the exit. Lily was still crying, but the tone of the wails had subsided to a more pitiful resignation. "We have to find some sterile water, a way to clean these bottles, and then feed her."

"I'll take care of it." Grayson was wearing that intense expression again. He directed her out the door and back to the SUV, watching their surroundings with a practiced case. She felt safe, despite the situation, with him towering behind her.

He drove them to a small strip mall, pulled in close to the back door of a restaurant and ordered her to stay put while he hopped out, keeping the SUV in sight with his body turned at a slight angle. He went to the door and spoke briefly to someone before handing off the bottles.

Lauren took in their surroundings. The clouds had not dissipated, making things shadowy and still. They were parked between a convenience store and the restaurant. Her stomach growled and she realized that Grayson, too, was probably hungry. She longed to make a break for it to retrieve some snacks until they could stop for more food. Maybe she could talk him into going inside the restaurant once they had sterilized the bottles.

Lily had calmed now that she was at least comfortably dressed and was working a pacifier. Grayson returned to a position nearer the SUV, waiting for the bottles, so Lauren decided to give Lily a break from the car seat. There was not another soul around, so she slid from the passenger seat and moved to the back seat to unbuckle the infant.

She pulled Lily from the carrier and tucked her up against her chest. She slid out of the back seat with her before turning to find Grayson watching her with an angry expression.

"What are you doing?"

Lauren shrugged. "I thought Lily might be happy to get out of that seat for a little while. You made it sound like we have a long way to go before we get settled."

"You shouldn't have her out in the open like this. Someone could be watching." He ushered her back toward the vehicle.

"Actually, I'm pretty hungry. Do you think we could go into that store and get some snacks while we wait for the bottles?" Lauren gestured in the direction of the convenience store.

He didn't look especially pleased but nodded his assent. "We will have to make it quick. The woman will be back with the bottles soon."

They ducked into the store and Lauren gathered a few things up with one hand, cradling Lily with the other. Grayson watched the door carefully as she went to the counter to pay.

Grayson followed her outside, collar drawn up around his face. Lauren turned to see not the woman she'd expected, but a burly man coming out of the back of the restaurant with the bottles. Her gut twisted.

Something wasn't right.

Grayson must have felt the same way as he ordered the man to set down the bottles and go back inside. He reached for his gun but wasn't quick enough. The man tossed the plastic bottles and lunged at him in one swift movement.

Grayson reacted quickly, working the man over with his fists in self-defense, but not before another man appeared closer to Lauren.

Grayson fought hard to get away from his attacker, but the man was at least twice his size and not easily deterred.

Too far outside the store, Lauren picked up her pace as the wind hit her face. The man's shadow fell across the sidewalk despite the overcast sky. Her skin prickled in cold fear. She started to run, cradling Lily carefully as she did, but before she could get to the SUV, the footsteps sounded close behind her.

And a gloved hand grazed her shoulder.

THREE

Lauren tried not to panic.

The shadow had overtaken her and was grasping for her. She lunged away from him, narrowly missing his grip before fleeing.

The rush of rapidly moving blood flowing through her veins filled her ears. How could she and Lily have so easily become separated from Grayson? They had managed the shopping without any problems. She had been so vigilant about staying with him.

There was no one in sight to help them, just the man in the dark hood coming toward Lauren and Lily. She had lost sight of Grayson, with the hooded man filling her vision. The buildings around them blocked her view of anyone else, as well. There was little traffic and the city streets were quiet. It seemed like an unpopular area. It had been a mistake to stop here. She thought a city would be safe, but the out-of-the-way mall provided too much opportunity for their pursuer.

When she realized she was trapped and couldn't reach the SUV in time, she tried to move back toward the restaurant where she had last seen Grayson, but the hooded man was between them. She should have been on constant watch. This shouldn't be happening.

Lily began to fuss, and Lauren let her, thinking it might not be a bad thing if the baby's cries drew some attention. Lauren, too, cried out, Grayson's name sounding hollow and too weak coming from her dry throat. Footsteps sounded in the distance. Lauren held her breath, but no one appeared.

The man in the hood crept closer, like a shadowy villain from a comic strip, moving with almost no sound toward where she stood. Lauren backed away, unwilling to let him gain any advantage. The shadows deepened around them as the clouds seemed to thicken over the sun, and Lauren felt a scream bubbling up within her chest as the hooded man charged at them.

"Lauren!" Grayson's voice echoed toward her finally. His footfalls were close now.

"Here!" She ducked out of the way. The hooded man narrowly missed grasping her and clamping a hand over her mouth. Her attacker dived at her again and pushed her to the ground. She let out a gasp of dismay, trying to keep Lily securely against her chest to protect her from the impact as she tumbled toward the sidewalk.

He growled and tried to snatch the baby from her grasp, but Lauren gripped her tighter and turned away from his clutching paws. She kicked at him as she cradled the child. Lily was crying in earnest now, making Lauren more anxious. Lauren knew Grayson was close, because the last time she had caught a glimpse of him, he was headed toward them. He wouldn't let them get far. She cried out again. The stench of the nearby dumpsters and exhaust from earlier traffic mingled to make her gag.

"Grayson! Help!" She gasped again, tasting her fear on the indrawn breath.

With one last attempt to wrest the baby from her grasp, the man gave up. Throwing a look over his shoulder at Grayson, he turned and fled. Grayson pursued him for a little ways while Lauren eased to her feet, holding Lily's soft body to her the whole time. She was barely upright by the time he was back at her side.

"He's gone." Grayson grunted out the words as he helped Lauren check on the baby in her arms. Lily sent out a serious howl and Lauren tried to comfort her with gentle whispers and small rocking motions. Other than hunger and upset, the infant seemed to be unharmed.

"I'm sorry." Lauren whispered the words to him. "This was a terrible idea. I shouldn't have insisted we stop."

He pressed his lips together. "It was my final decision. It's not your fault. I thought we had lost them for a bit. Are you okay?"

She nodded, trying not to let him see how frightened she was. She could handle herself if it came down to her own survival. But being responsible for Lily was scary.

"Look at me, Lauren." She did so when his deep voice penetrated the fog of fear surrounding her.

"I'm fine." She felt like a child, squeaking out the words. "*We're* fine."

"Yes." He watched her face, studied her, eyes roaming and probing her own. "Yes, you are both fine."

She shivered. "I'm sorry, Grayson. I'm so sorry."

He reached for Lily. "Let me see her."

When she handed her over, the baby's cries settled. She had sensed Lauren's upset. Honestly, Lauren was a little envious of the comfort Lily was receiving in Grayson's strong arms. It was an unwanted emotion that came to her without warning.

She shook off the thoughts with a jolt. There was no room for that sort of thinking between them. She couldn't allow herself to think like that about him. Not about any man, but especially not Grayson. She was nothing to him. He was just doing a job. She sensed he wouldn't welcome those kinds of feelings from her. She had never been the kind of woman to inspire love and commitment from handsome men.

"Lauren?" he asked, still looking at the baby.

"Hmm?" She turned her eyes back to the infant, as well, wondering what he was studying there.

"You have nothing to be sorry for." He held out a hand.

She took it, bracing herself against the warmth and comfort she found there. "Are you sure?"

"I'm sure." He looked at her face at last. She sensed something behind his eyes, a battle within his emotions, as well. Was she misreading it? Surely she was wrong. She should have learned by now that she was too trusting, too ready to believe the best in people.

She nodded.

"Can you walk back?" He returned his focus to the baby.

"Yes. I'll be fine." She let go of his hand and picked up the sack she had dropped when trying to protect Lily.

He frowned. "Then we'd better get going before he decides to return with reinforcements."

Once they made it back to the SUV and were headed out of town again, Lauren asked the question she had been wondering. "How?"

He gripped the wheel tighter. "How did he find us?"

"Mmm-hmm." She bit her lip. "You turned off my phone. How could they track us?"

He let out a little chuckle. "You're never going to forgive me for the phone, are you?"

She gave a half shrug. A tiny grin fought to appear, though. "Maybe. One day."

"Well…" He paused, turned down the radio and then gave a little grin in return. "I'll make it up to you sometime. And as for how, I don't really know. I have a GPS blocker installed in my SUV, the kind the military uses. I have no idea how they found us."

Lauren looked at him for a moment before nodding her acceptance of his answer. "So they can probably find us again."

His reply was almost too quiet. "Probably. I'm going to do a thorough search of the vehicle to make sure they haven't installed another device while I was inside the hospital. It could be they have one advanced enough to override my GPS blocker somehow."

"Next time someone tries to snatch Lily, I'll be ready."

He let out a sound that was a lot like a growl. "I plan to see to it that there isn't a next time. They won't get between us again."

Once they were sure their ambushers were gone, Lauren climbed over the narrow console and into the back of the SUV to feed Lily. It was obvious the little one was more than ready to eat; she attacked the bottle with noisy smacks that made Lauren smile.

Grayson had found a secure place to stop down the road a ways, where he searched the vehicle for GPS blockers while Lauren had seen to getting the bottles sterilized again, this time under watch of several local officers who had responded to the call. He had found nothing, which he didn't seem surprised by, and when Lauren had coaxed the gas from Lily's tummy and settled her into the seat, he had sighed in relief.

Now it was all still and quiet. Lily had gone to sleep almost as soon as the SUV began to move, and Lauren felt too alone with Grayson once more. The food seemed unimportant now. In fact, she couldn't even think of eating with her stomach churning as it was.

Grayson had chosen a two-lane highway as they drove out of town, rather than stick with the predictable and highly visible interstate. She felt a little isolated on the lonely road, but assumed he knew best given the circumstances.

She tried to think of something mundane to discuss, anything that might turn their thoughts away from their predicament, but nothing came to mind. While she could ask questions to learn more about him, she didn't have a clue where to start. So she sat silently in her insecurity.

Grayson didn't seem to notice, focusing on the road ahead with smoky-blue eyes that were almost unseeing. His hand was on his chest again. He did that a lot. No doubt his thoughts were occupied with doing his job. She wished hers could be so easily contained.

Worry over her job, her family and protecting Lily warred for dominance. And there was always the fear that they might have missed something with Lily's health. She seemed all right, but it wasn't unheard of that something might surface later.

She thought back to cases of such instances that she knew of, but Lily had no symptoms. Actually, she seemed healthier than many full-term babies. She had a perfect pink color about her, strong lungs and above-average developmental skills, and her Apgar score had been perfect. As a NICU nurse, it was important that she know what was normal for a newborn, especially a preemie. She saw all degrees of health in infants daily, and Lily was one of the healthiest she had ever seen. It almost seemed that, despite modern technology, the obstetrician had simply miscalculated her due date.

"That's it." Lauren gasped the words out loud,

which she didn't realize until Grayson looked at her in surprise.

"What's it?" Grayson turned his attention back to the road.

"I don't think Lily was early. It was a misdiagnosis." The confidence and strength in her voice sounded so different from the timidity of the moment before.

"A misdiagnosis?" He looked perplexed.

"Well…no, maybe not that, exactly. But they recorded the wrong due date. It was intended to throw everyone off. If whoever was trying to kidnap her thought the baby wasn't due until much later, it would give Lily's mother time to escape with her before he realized the baby had been born. She expected the baby to be in danger all along."

"But someone failed to inform the hospital staff that the due date was a ruse." Grayson raised an eyebrow. "That meant the baby was kept for observation and Savannah couldn't leave with her."

"That's exactly what happened. I think she had an on-call obstetrician for delivery." Lauren thought carefully.

"That would have ruined their plan." He rubbed a forefinger against his lower lip.

"So Lily's mother probably had a good relationship with Dr. Worman, her OB. Maybe we can use that information to help us find her." Lauren reached for her phone before remembering she didn't have it.

"What's wrong?"

"I don't have a phone to call to find out her OB's number from Dr. Covington." She glared at him.

"Oh. That." He just stared ahead.

"I can't help you if you're going to be obstinate," she muttered.

"Well, you can use mine. Or you can call when we get to the safe house." He just shrugged.

"Any idea when that might be?" They had been driving for hours. She wanted to demand answers but didn't think that would get her anywhere with Grayson Thorpe.

"Still awaiting orders." He checked his phone for any messages before handing it to her.

"So, you're just driving. Driving southwest until someone tells you where to go." She couldn't fathom doing something like that with no plan in mind whatsoever.

"That's what I was told to do." He seemed unperturbed by the fact.

She sighed. He wasn't going to tell her anything.

"We're trying to get lost anyway." He just shrugged. "What's the big deal?"

"Well, it just doesn't make sense." She crossed her arms and shook her head. Obstinate man.

She turned away from him, settled into the seat and tried to pretend to sleep.

* * *

Lauren wasn't fooling anyone.

Grayson hadn't meant to argue with her, but now that he had, she wasn't going to forget it anytime soon. It was obvious she intended to feign sleep to avoid him because she couldn't physically get away from him.

She had no idea how it had panicked him when that man had accosted her and Lily outside the restaurant. He felt he had let her down, that he should have been more prepared for an attack. Lauren had handled it well. She hadn't complained since they'd left the hospital, and he had a feeling she was accustomed to taking care of herself.

When the man had knocked her down and she had rolled sideways and curled herself into a ball to take the full brunt of the impact and protect the baby, he had known she was a special kind of woman. He hadn't even noticed the scrape along her high cheekbone until later as she gently coaxed the bottle into the baby's tiny mouth.

Lily had been so upset by her ordeal that she hadn't even wanted to take the bottle at first, but with the expertise born of years of practice, Lauren had eventually convinced her to drink. He kept remembering Lauren's soft urging, thinking how right she looked with the child, like a natural mother.

It was a mind trick, of course. She was a NICU

nurse. She was an expert with newborns. And he was an expert at bachelorhood, which was how it would stay. He had learned that he was better off alone after almost getting his whole team killed because of a woman. His current feelings were nothing but the result of being thrown together like this.

Grayson turned his thoughts in another direction. It would take a huge amount of concentration, but he had to figure out where they might have taken Lily's mother. He needed to talk to Savannah to find out who was after Lily and why. He had received a text from his supervisor just before the attack at the restaurant. He was sending them toward Texas. But he didn't know where, exactly, so he didn't want to say so to Lauren.

If Grayson wasn't mistaken, Lily's mother had family or friends in Texas. He knew his supervisor felt Savannah Reid was the key to capturing Arnie Romine, whether he was behind the kidnapping attempts or not. It was all one big, complicated case.

The files had indicated that Savannah had known nothing about Romine, or even who he really was, when they'd first met. Grayson suspected Romine had known all about Savannah and had planned an elaborate scheme to use her somehow. But—trite as it sounded—he seemed to have fallen in love with her along the way. Grayson wasn't sure about that, but it was the general belief. Maybe Romine was just a fantastic actor. Love was just an illusion most of the time anyway. An illusion that could get you into trouble.

He tried to accept the idea of true love. Really, he did. He went to church. He prayed. He knew about real love. But romantic love between a man and a woman was hard for him to believe in. He had seen too many cases of love gone wrong, one half of the relationship caring more than the other, and so on. He just didn't think he wanted any part of that.

The back of his neck began to itch, chasing all thoughts of romance from his mind. Looking over at Lauren, he realized she had actually gone to sleep, her delicate features relaxed and soft. At least her stubbornness was good for something. She needed to rest.

But she had nothing to do with the reason he felt a sudden trip in his adrenaline.

Checking his mirrors, he saw nothing amiss. He kept driving, noting the changing landscape as they passed. He had been lost in thought and now didn't know for sure exactly where they were, but his pursuers didn't have any such issues keeping track of where they were. They were nearly impossible to lose. In fact, he expected them to reappear any moment.

The trees had gotten thicker and taller in this

area, as well. He knew they had risen in elevation slightly, and tall pines were becoming a regular sight. The cover didn't do them much good if their pursuers already knew where they were, though. And the way they kept showing up told him that they somehow knew his every move.

He glanced down to check his phone for messages, in case there was more information from headquarters, quickly returning his eyes to the road. It would be nice to have Lauren's help right about now, but he wouldn't wake her unless he just had to.

They weren't far from the interstate. Glancing at the map on the screen of his GPS, he discovered the two roads would intersect soon. It might be a good idea to return to the busier highway for a little while.

Grayson still didn't know how their pursuers were tracking them, but he felt certain they were just waiting on another chance to attack. Their current surroundings were looking a little too much like a good opportunity to suit him.

Lily made a sweet little baby noise in her sleep and it spurred him into action. He needed to do something soon before it was too late.

He accelerated, pressing his foot down hard on the gas pedal. The less time spent in this shady area, the better, as far as he was concerned.

Lauren shifted a little but didn't rise. He adjusted the air vents so that she wouldn't get too chilled. He could turn the temperature up, but he needed to stay alert and keep his blood flowing. He checked his mirrors again. Nothing.

But the neck itches persisted.

Something was about to happen. The anticipation combined with not knowing tormented him.

The highway remained empty, both in front and behind them, which had Grayson scanning the tree line. The tall pines had grown thicker on either side of the road and they seemed to be winding up a small mountain or large hill. It was serene. Peaceful. Beautiful.

Too quiet.

His cell rang, loud in the silence, startling him more than it should have.

"Thorpe." He barked his name into the Bluetooth speaker a little sharper than usual.

"Hey, buddy. I've got your orders. Can you verify you've received the address in your GPS?"

Cane Mason was one of Grayson's oldest friends, not just in the Marshals Service, but ever. No way did Grayson believe he hadn't noticed his sharp tone.

"Yeah. But maybe not at this exact moment."

"Uh… I know you didn't answer with someone in pursuit. You would have let it go to voice mail, like always. What's up?" Cane chuckled.

"Oh, you know. Just that something's-about-to-happen feeling when you're alone on a deserted two-lane highway in the middle of nowhere." Grayson sounded nonchalant, but every marshal knew it was a moment you both lived for and dreaded.

Impending doom.

"Gotcha. So, do I need to just stay on the line or…?" Cane sounded almost envious.

"Unless you have something more pressing to do, I can tell you what's happened so far while we wait." He checked the mirrors again and then looked over to ensure Lauren was still asleep.

"Yeah, I'm all caught up on paperwork for the day. I need answers to some questions." Cane's voice came through a little rougher than it had before.

"I'm sure you have questions. But sometimes things don't go exactly as planned." Grayson sensed his questions had something to do with Grayson's bringing Lauren along.

Cane was silent for a moment. "So, not a good time. Is there anything I can do?"

"I have it under control at the moment, but thanks." His words came out more chipper than usual.

But they were still echoing back to him when he rounded the corner and discovered what all the itchy, prickly feels were about.

Three black vans blocked the road.

FOUR

The vans were wedged between a thick stand of trees on one side and a cliff-like drop-off on the other. There was absolutely nowhere for him to go.

"Cane?" Grayson said the name so quietly he almost couldn't be heard. "I have a problem."

Even as he said it, he slammed on the brakes. If he had room, stopping in time to turn around would be tough. The antilock brakes caught and slid before catching again. He kept his foot depressed hard on the pedal. The baby started to fuss, and Lauren jerked to attention.

The SUV began to slide to one side and he gripped the wheel, mentally scrolling through every defensive driving maneuver he had ever been taught for what he needed. He couldn't think of anything that would possibly get him turned around and moving in the opposite direction quickly enough.

"What's going on?" Lauren was alert but confused.

"Roadblock. Hold on." He was turning the SUV

in a circle, doing his best to block out the baby's cries. He knew Lauren would take care of Lily as soon as she could, but his blood pressure spiked higher the louder the baby wailed.

He had never had anything throw off his calm like a crying baby. It bothered him, the fact that he was losing his cool. He had been telling the truth when he'd told Lauren he had never been around small children. At first, it was just how it worked out, since he never had the opportunity to be around babies anyway, but the few times he had been around them, he'd felt awkward, inadequate. So he had learned to avoid anyone under the age of two...

He still felt inadequate. Maybe helpless was more like it. Whatever it was, his ego had no use for it.

Might as well do what he could to help his confidence, though, so he wheeled the SUV with no time to spare and gunned it in the other direction. Just as he knew they would, all three vans gave chase. They sped closer, trying to close off his avenue of escape. This situation was all too familiar.

Lauren was singing to the baby, but it was having no effect on Lily's cries.

"Just let her cry. I'll get us out of here."

Lauren winced at the baby's piercing screams. "Okay. I just thought it would help you concentrate if I could quiet her."

He was that obvious, huh? "It'll be okay."

She nodded. Her attention was drawn to the black van pulling up alongside as they cruised along a wide, flat stretch of road. Another van advanced on the driver's side as a third van closed in on their rear bumper.

"Cute, guys. Real cute. But I don't think so." Grayson floored it, and the SUV shot forward and away from the vans. Just in time, a semi topped the hill from the opposite direction, scattering the vans into a line behind him.

He flashed his lights at the semi and the truck driver slowed as Grayson checked in with Cane. "You still there, buddy?"

"I'm sending backup to your location. Just stay smart and hold tight." Cane sounded distracted, clearly taking care of the details even as he spoke.

"You're the best, bro." He nodded at Lauren. "You can jump back there with the baby now, but make it fast." She wasted no time scrambling into the back seat.

As the semi passed, he gunned it once more, fully expecting the three vans to try again. "Hold on tight, Lauren. I'm going to be taking some of these turns as fast as I can to try to get rid of these guys long enough for help to get here."

The vans accelerated, also, but the SUV was more powerful, putting some distance between them.

Lauren was soothing the baby as best she could,

but it looked as though her nerves were fraying. Lily had quieted a little, but still emitted some pitiful cries here and there. He might have to stop sooner than he'd planned just to calm them all.

"Cane?" Grayson knew his buddy was still on the line, even though he had gone silent, probably listening in.

"Here, bro." Cane's calm reassured Grayson that he was about to get help.

"Can you tell me how far we are from the destination?" He didn't like the weariness in his voice.

"Farther than you'd like, I'm sure. Let me ping your location and calculate it." The line went silent for a moment. "Looks like about four and a half hours."

Grayson bit back an ugly reply. "All right. I'm going to need to stop before then."

The SUV was blanketed in quiet before Cane's voice came through the Bluetooth speaker system once more. "Are you okay?"

"Yeah. We just all need out of this vehicle for a little bit. Traveling with a baby is…different." He couldn't say it was difficult with Lauren listening in. His ego was already taking a hit at his inability to take care of the baby.

"Oh, I'm sure that's an understatement." Cane laughed. "It looks like there is a town up ahead that should be safe enough for you to stop and take a stretch, as long as we can lose your tails."

"I see blue lights just ahead now." Relief filled Grayson as the three black vans slowed their advance. "Thanks, Cane."

"Not a problem. Stop in Barnesdale if you can. It looks to be a safe bet. If you need me, just call."

Grayson made a sound of agreement and Cane disconnected. The vans had dropped way back by the time the flashing lights reached Grayson's SUV. He waved at the troopers and kept driving, watching in his rearview mirror as they passed the semi and headed for his chasers. The vans turned off in different directions, but the troopers followed. He knew they probably wouldn't discover much if they caught up with his pursuers, but at least they would keep the bad guys busy for a while.

Grayson checked his GPS to see that Cane had sent the info to take them to the town of Barnesdale. As soon as they got there, he pulled into a kid-friendly restaurant and followed the females inside. When Lauren and Lily were situated and safe, he called Cane back to get his orders.

When Cane gave him the location of the safe house, Grayson didn't say anything, just grunted. Cane read him like only a longtime friend could.

"You aren't happy to be going back to Oklahoma? You know it's one of the safest places in the country." Cane chuckled. "Mostly because there isn't much going on there."

"Yeah. I mean, that much is true. At least tell me it's a long way from that last hideout we had to endure. If I run into those busybodies from the last town in Oklahoma, I might have to quit my job." Grayson grumbled the words, hoping Lauren didn't hear. He definitely didn't want to run into anyone who might know Rebecca.

Cane laughed again. He didn't know the whole story. Grayson had gone to great lengths to make sure no one knew all the embarrassing details. "No worries. You'll be on the other side of the state. But I can't promise there won't be more sweet old ladies looking out for your welfare."

The local church ladies in the last Oklahoma town had been so determined to see him happily matched that they had almost ruined the whole mission. Cane thought it was a hilarious joke. Grayson was glad his friend didn't know the church ladies' matchmaking scheme had played right into Rebecca's hands. "Not funny, bro."

"If it helps, it's near a lake. Up in the hills." Cane had at least stopped laughing.

"Fantastic. 'Cause hiding out beside a lake with a baby, watching other people wakeboard and ride Jet Skis, sounds like an awesome time." Grayson infused fake cheer into his sarcasm.

"Oh, come on. You are being paid for this, so complaining is pretty pointless."

"Sure. Well, I'd better get back to it." Grayson ignored Cane's renewed laughter as he disconnected.

Lauren read his expression too accurately. "It isn't good news?"

"Not for me. Maybe you will like Oklahoma." Grayson did little to hide his grimace.

"I've never been there. I wouldn't know." She glanced at Lily. "I've never been farther west than Tennessee. I've spent most of my life pretty close to DC."

He didn't know how to react to that. He really had completely upended her life. "Well, I guess this is your chance."

She was so quiet he began to wonder what she was thinking. "You might like it. It's a whole lot different than DC."

"But you don't like it." She didn't have to ask. Her tone implied she already knew his answer.

"I-it's fine." He wasn't about to tell her about Oklahoma right now. If he had his preference, he would never talk to anyone about it. Ever. That was where he'd met Rebecca, the woman who had almost cost him his life and the lives of his men. He couldn't tell her about the church ladies without mentioning Rebecca.

"Oh, it's fine, huh? That sounds promising." She probably would have crossed her arms over her chest if she hadn't been holding Lily. He noticed her eyes were moving around the room, almost as if she was looking for danger in every corner.

He hoped she would forget it. He wasn't at all ready to talk to her about something so personal.

He glanced around at the brightly colored tables and booths, thinking their surroundings were way too cheerful for the situation. It made him a little angry. The two females across the table from him didn't deserve this.

"Look, I'll try to get you out of there as soon as I possibly can. Besides, it isn't like we're going to be out seeing the sights." It came out a little gruffer than he'd intended, and she blinked at him in surprise.

"Okay. Yeah, I guess that's true. It doesn't really matter if we like it there or not. What matters is keeping Lily safe."

As if her words had renewed the danger somehow, a shadow beyond the huge pane of glass caught his attention. On the grass just past the parking lot, there was a man standing beside a tree, and he was trying not to be caught watching them. Grayson already knew, though.

"Lauren? I want you to slowly and casually gather all the baby's things and act like you are heading to the women's restroom." He spoke in a calm, quiet voice.

"What? Why?" Lauren followed his gaze.

"Don't look. You'll give us away. Just do it.

Calmly. I'll be right there." He kept his eyes on her face.

"In the ladies' room?" Her voice squeaked and he laughed.

"No, but right outside. When it's safe, we're going to get out of here." He nodded as if to acknowledge her intent to go to the ladies' room, for the benefit of their observer.

Lauren only hesitated a moment before taking her cue, faintly trembling as she grasped the new diaper bag and slung it onto her shoulder. She strode purposefully toward the bathroom and he tried to watch the man's reaction without being obvious. The lanky observer flicked a cigarette onto the grass at his feet before making his way to the restaurant.

Grayson waited until he knew the man could no longer see him and then he moved quickly. He muttered gruff apologies to a few people that he hurried past on his way to reach Lauren and Lily before the other man could. An elderly woman with a walker, however, proved to be a bigger obstacle than he'd expected. He held in a sigh, gently assisting her with her walker before practically sprinting to the ladies' room. He had lost sight of the man who had been watching them.

He slowed and turned to look for the man again. He didn't see him, even though there wasn't much to impede his view, with the small number of patrons present. Deciding to continue on around the corner to get to Lauren and Lily, he turned and directly collided with the man he had been searching for.

"Hey! Watch where you're going, man," the guy growled at Grayson as he stumbled hard.

Grayson didn't back down. He pulled out his badge. "US marshal. Official business."

The man's eyes bulged momentarily before he could hide his reaction. "Oh, right. Sorry to get in your way."

Grayson moved on toward the ladies' room to stand guard, pretending not to notice how the man slunk away in the other direction. Hadn't he known what he was up against? Or had he just thought he was slick enough to pull off a kidnapping right under Grayson's nose?

Since the man was just a hired kidnapper, it was likely no one had told him what he was getting into. Whoever had sent him had probably just told him he would be paid to bring them the baby.

"You okay?" Grayson cracked open the door to the ladies' room, turned his face away and stuck his foot in to wait for a reply. He didn't have to wait long.

"Yes. Can we come out?" Lauren sounded breathless and a little shaky.

"Stay put for just a minute. I want to make sure he's really gone."

Grayson let the door bump shut as he made his way along the small corridor to the closest window. The man was getting into an old, beaten-looking sedan. There was a middle-aged woman sitting in the front passenger seat. Grayson would need to be on his guard for her, as well, so he noted everything he could about the woman. She had stringy, dirty blond hair and was slightly overweight. He couldn't distinguish much about her features behind the windshield's glare, other than she had small, deep-set eyes and scabs on both cheeks, as if she suffered from acne or some other skin condition. She flicked a cigarette out the window and he immediately recalled the stench of the things. It filled him with nausea, even as he tried to suppress the memories.

He touched his chest absently. The raised scar was still there, but it was smaller. He would always have that horrible reminder of his failure.

"Is everything okay?" Lauren had appeared beside him, completely unnoticed, and stood holding Lily to her chest as naturally as any practiced mother. She was so close he could smell her unique exotic scent. How had he not noticed her presence sooner?

"I thought I told you to stay put." He might have spoken too harshly, if her step back was any indication.

"You did. I'm sorry. Is he gone?" Her tone held

nothing to betray any remorse. And she offered no explanation.

"Yeah. Yeah, he is." He just stared at her for a moment. To his surprise, she returned the stare and never flinched. She didn't ask for any answers. She didn't demand. She didn't offer any more apologies. She just waited.

It really messed with him. "Well, we'd better get moving."

Without reply, she turned and did as he asked. It took him a moment to follow. She was so different from the girls—women—he was accustomed to being around.

She had Lily in the car seat by the time he reached the SUV and climbed in behind the wheel. She was sitting beside the baby in the back seat.

He frowned at her in the rearview mirror. "You're sitting back there?"

"It's almost time for her to have another feeding. I didn't think you'd want to stop again." She buckled her seat belt.

Oh. Right. "Well, thanks, but we can stop if we need to. Just let me know. How is she doing?" he asked as he briefly glanced away and then back.

"I have tried to monitor her vitals manually at regular intervals, taking her pulse by hand, and I did snatch a blood pressure cuff and thermometer, but there has been a lot going on. She seems healthy, though. Only an occasional cough." Lauren pulled a notepad from her purse to show him. "I'm having to keep track by hand, though."

Another dig at him about the cell phone. She just wasn't going to let that go. "Is the cough cause for any concern?"

"Not unless she develops other symptoms, such as fever, shortness of breath or wheezing. Any newborn is at a fairly high risk for respiratory syncytial virus, or RSV, but if she is premature, she is at an even greater risk, as well as at a high risk for pneumonia. The virus can cause inflammation of the airways in one so young. And bronchiolitis and severe cold-like symptoms. They usually lead to other complications in infants. It's not easy to manage, sometimes requiring hospitalization and breathing treatments." Lauren put the notepad in her handbag.

"That doesn't sound good. But you know what to watch for." He was stating the obvious again. Having a baby to protect was completely out of his realm of expertise.

"Yes, of course. An occasional cough could be just her clearing her lungs from the birth. It's normal for all babies to cough once in a while. Just like adults, the problems have other symptoms, while a cough alone could just be a little tickle." She was giving him the patient look a woman might give a child as she explained something.

He found he didn't really want her to look at him like that. It was a blow to his ego.

"Right. Well, you do your thing and I'll do mine. You keep her healthy and I'll keep her safe." He tried but couldn't miss the expression on her face. What he really wished he could have missed was the hurt. He turned on the radio before she could reply.

He couldn't tell her about the bad decisions he'd made in the past because he had caught feelings for someone.

He didn't look away until she did. The hurt, however, didn't leave her face even when she focused on Lily. The regret he felt surprised him. Shutting someone out was harder than he'd expected, even though he had little choice. He couldn't let his past mistakes be repeated, even if Lauren seemed to be much different from Rebecca.

The SUV remained far too quiet for the next couple of hours. But Grayson could find no way to take back what he had said. Every time he thought he might have found the words, they got stuck in his throat. Yet thoughts of how he could fix it never completely left him.

His phone rang through the Bluetooth system, startling them both, apparently, because Lauren jumped. Lily began to fuss, aroused from her sleep, but Lauren's soothing almost immediately calmed the infant.

Grayson tapped the answer button and said his name before the phone could ring again.

There was a long pause at the other end.

"Hello?" He repeated his name and waited, but only a brief silence ensued before a click indicated the caller was gone.

He growled his displeasure.

"Do you think it was the kidnapper? Trying to bargain for the baby?" Lauren asked hesitantly.

"He couldn't possibly have gotten this number. Probably a mistake." Grayson tried to blow it off. But he, too, wondered what was going on.

"I'm sure you're right. I'm new at this. I might have watched too many scary movies as a teenager." She laughed, but he didn't. He was too busy picturing her as a teenager. Had her years been as serious as his own at that point, or had she been bubbly and full of life?

He dismissed the thoughts, wishing he had never consented to them.

"I don't know why he would call and hang—"

At that moment, the phone rang again.

"Thorpe."

"Marshal Thorpe, this is Senator Reid. I understand you have been assigned protective custody of my newly arrived granddaughter."

The voice was authoritative, self-assured. Knowing him to be a no-nonsense, too-busy-to-waste-time type of man, Grayson figured the senator had probably been the one to hang up, likely because something more important had come along.

"You've been informed correctly, sir. What can I do for you?" Grayson did his best to keep his tone even and amicable. It wasn't his first instinct. He tried not to allow what he had heard about the senator to color his response.

"You can keep her out of that despicable man's grasp. If he gets his hands on her, he will do a terrible job of trying to make me pay. I'm in no mood to have my grandchild taken for ransom, and things could get ugly. I wouldn't say I would take it out on you, exactly, but you might lose my support for your government-appointed position." The man's voice sounded much more conciliatory than his words implied.

"Of course, Senator. I will see to it that she is kept safe and out of harm's way. You worry about finding her mother until this is over. I'm sure you're terribly worried about her." Grayson didn't let on how offensive he found the man's threats. He was a powerful man that Grayson wasn't in a hurry to anger.

"My daughter?" Genuine confusion filled the senator's tone. "What are you talking about?"

"Savannah? I assume there is no news about her kidnapping?" Grayson had hoped that somehow Senator Reid might know something about his daughter's disappearance. But it seemed he wasn't even aware that she was missing.

"I thought Savannah was with you and the baby. I haven't heard anything." There was an edge of anger in his voice now. "Who is taking care of the child? You surely aren't alone with her."

"Never mind that, sir. She is well taken care of. But we do need to locate her mother. There is another marshal on the case searching for her, but she disappeared from the hospital a little before I arrived. The security guard said there were signs of a struggle. It seems the marshal protecting her was attacked. Do you know of any reason someone might have taken her?" Grayson cut his gaze to Lauren in the rearview mirror. She was listening intently, her eyes wide and mouth slack. He couldn't imagine what she must be feeling.

"There are any number of people who could have kidnapped her, I suppose. To attempt to get money from me or because of her own unfortunate decisions." The senator's tone conveyed little sympathy for his daughter. "I'll see what I can find out."

Grayson gave him the number of the marshal working on Savannah's disappearance. The senator took it wordlessly without a mention of thanks. "Keep me updated on my granddaughter."

The line disconnected.

"Wow." Lauren's statement echoed his thoughts. He clenched his jaw. "This case keeps getting more complicated by the second."

FIVE

Lauren would have declared *relief* far too mild a sentiment to name what she was feeling when they finally arrived at the safe house. It was one thing to spend hours caring for newborns in a hospital setting, but it was much different to try to do so while running from kidnappers.

Just as Grayson's friend had promised, the house was beside a beautiful, tranquil lake and surrounded by huge trees and lush vegetation. Everything was green and smelled so fresh and clean she wanted to breathe more deeply each time.

"Careful. You'll hyperventilate." He didn't even crack a grin, but she knew it was a joke. She was beginning to sense the humor behind his tough veneer.

"It smells almost as wonderful as it looks." Lauren stepped around the SUV to get a better look at the house. "Oh, wow."

It was a beautiful, two-story log cabin. It had dormer windows along the second-story roofline and a front porch that stretched the length of the home. Moss green shutters framed the windows and cedar-shake shingles finished off the natural look. A rolling green lawn disappeared into stately oak and pines. A glimpse of blue-green water shimmered in the distance through the trees.

"I might never want to leave." Her words sounded breathy and awed, even to herself. She hoped he didn't sense the turn her thoughts had taken without even trying. The three of them, as a family, coming to such a place for a vacation flitted into her mind before she could stop it. She pushed it away.

He seemed amused by her comment. "I wouldn't have guessed you to be the outdoorsy type."

"I've never really been given the chance." She realized the truth of it when she said it.

His expression was one of surprise. "You've never been camping?"

She gave a short, self-deprecating laugh. "My family was never big on vacations and outings. In fact, we didn't spend a great deal of time together."

He frowned, but she didn't want his pity. Her dysfunctional family had made her who she was today. Her life was firmly rooted in her Christian faith. The church had become her family in ways her biological family never had been. She had been close to her father before he died, but she'd also been young at the time. She and her sister had only actually become close recently.

"I was an only child for a long time." She blurted it out as if that explained everything. It didn't, of course.

"Oh. Well, you should appreciate that. I grew up with four brothers." His crooked grin said he was only half teasing.

"I would have loved to have had a brother." She couldn't keep the wistfulness from her tone.

He laughed. "Yeah, one, maybe. Four, no."

She laughed, too. "I mean, I guess I see your point. But anything would be better than none."

"I don't know about that." But he was smiling. She hoped he wasn't feeling sorry for her anymore.

"Can we see the inside of this beauty?" She gestured toward the house, then turned to remove Lily's infant carrier from its base.

"Cane said the key would be on the window ledge of the shop building behind the house. I'll go get it." He dashed around the side of the house.

Lauren gathered Lily's carrier and all her things. The sweet child barely sighed as Lauren lifted her from the SUV, her pink-rosebud mouth puckered and relaxed in tiny kisses. A pang of affection mixed with longing hit Lauren unexpectedly. She had taken care of a whole lot of babies in the NICU, but this feeling was something entirely new. Where had it come from?

She had clearly been stuck alone in the car with these two for far too long.

Grayson returned to find her mulling it over in stunned silence. "You okay?"

He cocked his head and it made him look almost boyish. His frown was different, too. Or was that her imagination? What was wrong with her?

"Um, yeah. I think I'm just tired from the drive." She smiled at him, but it felt weak.

She was thankful to be distracted by the interior of the home as Grayson swung open the door. The interior was just as charming as the exterior, cozy and neat. The descriptor "hygge" came to mind as she took in the comfy furnishings, fuzzy throws, pillows and soft rugs. The back of the house was primarily composed of windows that looked out over the sparkling lake, letting in a flood of light, even on a cloudy day.

"We'll have to work something out for Lily on a room. I realize the baby needs a safe place to sleep."

She nodded, trying to neutralize her expression. "Of course. So have you been in this house before? Do you know where we will put her?"

The impact began to sink in of the permanence of the situation. She realized they could be here indefinitely. He confirmed it with his response.

"I haven't been here before, so I thought we could decide together. I assume you'll want to put her bed in your room?" He directed her up the stairs and down a short hallway.

"Of course. I'd prefer to stay close to her at all times." The carrier shook a bit in her hand, and she looked down to see the blanket moving where Lily stirred beneath it. A tiny fist poked out. "It doesn't look like she's going to be patient much longer on her next feeding, though."

They began to look into each of the bedrooms. They were peeking into the last room when Lily began to fuss.

"This one will be the safest." His tone implied a final decision.

Lauren didn't like the fact that he didn't consult her. She tried to let it go but hated feeling controlled. It brought back too many unpleasant memories of her last relationship.

"Is there a problem with this room?" He must have read her hesitation.

She picked up on his slightly defensive tone. "I...want to be sure it is the best possible option. You said it's the safest. Why?"

He took a deep breath before he answered her. "It's farthest from the entrance, has the fewest windows and is accessible from the room across the hall, which is where I'll be."

"Hmm." She didn't say anything else, simply walked around the room, shushing Lily as she took in the details.

"What are you looking for?" He was frowning at her and held his arms crossed over his chest.

"Little things, actually. Just trying to decide if it's the best place for the baby. Where is the smoke alarm? The carbon monoxide detector? Do they work properly? It's a long way from the kitchen and living area downstairs. It might get to be a long trek for frequent bottle warmings."

"Those are all valid questions. I can check all the smoke alarms and carbon monoxide detectors tonight and make sure they are working. Hopefully, a baby monitor system can give you a little freedom. I purchased one when I bought the diapers. But I'd for sure like you to remain close to her at night." He was helping her scan the room now. "Is the distance to the kitchen a problem? I guess you're right. There will be a lot of bottles to warm."

"We can make do. If you believe this is the best possible option, we will be fine here." She settled the baby carrier on the bed and began to unfasten Lily from it. "I just wondered if that other room might be a better option. But it will work."

"Is there a problem with this room?" He crossed his arms over his chest once again.

"We can always make adjustments if we need to." She pulled out a diaper from the bag and began to change Lily, turning away from him. She could feel his stare against her back, though. She was weary from the endless hours of travel and the stress of the continual danger surrounding Lily. The energy to argue her point with him eluded her.

As Lily began to cry, he spoke. "I'll go see about warming a bottle."

"Thank you." She glanced over her shoulder at him.

Why was he so determined to put her in this room? Couldn't he at least ask for her input? Or did he just want control? The thought didn't exactly thrill her.

She had Lily swaddled and was rocking her back and forth while she waited on Grayson's return. It seemed to take him a long time. Restless, she wandered out of the room.

The room across the hall was slightly smaller, but it had a door leading to the bedroom beside it. She opened the door to the room next to what would be Grayson's, rocking Lily gently as she looked inside.

Lauren was still standing there, staring into the room, when Grayson walked down the hall. "What are you doing in here?" he asked from the doorway.

She turned to him. "Just looking around. Did you know these two rooms are adjoined?"

"No." He came into the room and handed her the warm bottle as he peered over her shoulder. "That could be pretty useful."

"Yes, but I'm sure it would have pitfalls, as well." She moved away from the door to feed the baby.

"True, but it would be helpful to be able to hear you and Lily, and to know if you needed help. You could leave the door cracked and…" He paused and looked at her. "I guess I should have considered this one before choosing the other one."

"I just thought we should weigh our options. If there is a reason the other room would be a more secure place for Lily, I can work with it." She watched Lily work at the bottle, making little gulping noises as she drank the formula.

He frowned. "From the outside, it seemed a better location because of the angle of the security cameras and the outdoor lights. Those are easily adjusted, if it makes you both more comfortable. I should have considered that this isn't a typical case. You and Lily need protection, but your comfort should have been a factor in my decision, as well. I guess I have a tendency just to take charge." He looked contrite as he cleared his throat. "Well, if you take the corner room, I'll take this adjoining room. The corner room has another window, but I'll adjust the security on that end of the house. Besides, it's on the second story. And it already has a smoke alarm and carbon monoxide detector."

She looked up at him and smiled. "That will be fine."

"I'll leave you to it, then." He nodded and ducked out of the room.

Lily gave a little coo, mouth full and eyes wide. "Oh, I know. I'm sure he will warm up to us both." Lauren giggled.

When Lily made another noise, Lauren nodded at her. "Yes, you'll have him charmed in no time. And we will just have to make the best of it until then."

As the baby finished the bottle, she began to drift off. Lauren continued to hold her as she walked to the window. The view was barely visible through the slightly open blinds. Even though outside it remained cloudy and dreary, the lake was a beautiful sight. Through the trees, she could see the blue water rippling in the bright sunshine. It was peaceful and calm. Lauren sighed as she twisted the rod on the blinds to tighten them closed all the way. She would rather have opened them to see out.

Under different circumstances, she would love being here. Growing up, her parents had always left her with her grandparents when they traveled. She had often dreamed of going camping when she was a child, but her mother and stepfather only vacationed in Europe or on the Caribbean islands—without her. When her sister was born, they'd stopped traveling altogether.

But she had let that go a long time ago, right?

She had given it over to God. It was all in the past, and that was where she should leave it.

Lauren pushed away the hurt. Her parents must have had good reasons for doing what they had. *Please, Lord, help me to let it go.*

One thing was sure, she thought as she looked down at Lily. If she were ever a mother, she would never do anything to make her child feel like an unwanted nuisance. When her baby sister had come along, after Lauren had turned fourteen, she had been unhappy at first. She'd enjoyed being an only child. But as she'd gotten older, things had changed. When she'd moved out of the family home, she had vowed to make sure Britlan never felt left out, even if it were just the two of them. If anything ever happened now, she would take on Britlan's care herself. But even if that never occurred, she would be there for her as much as she could.

Her thoughts led her to wonder about Lily's mother. Savannah knew she was in danger, but hadn't she realized the baby would be, as well? Lauren couldn't imagine how afraid for her Savannah must be, being kidnapped, leaving her child in the protection of strangers. It also seemed strange to her that someone had been able to get the drop on the marshal protecting her. It just didn't seem possible, considering no one should have known of her "early" delivery so quickly. Something about the scenario just didn't make sense.

She thought back to the conversation Grayson had had with Savannah Reid's father. Why wouldn't the Marshals Service have informed him of Savannah's kidnapping? Were they trying to keep from angering him, hoping they would find her before they had to do so? Or was there something more? And what about Savannah herself? Was no one looking for her?

Lauren heard footsteps and turned toward the door at Grayson's approach. "The view here is just amazing."

He nodded but seemed uninterested in small talk. "I thought you might be hungry. I can keep an eye on Lily if you want to eat. I made some pasta and garlic bread."

Lauren's eyebrows rose in surprise. Had she been standing around daydreaming so long? And he had *cooked*? "She's asleep. Maybe we could make her a pallet on the living room floor and eat together?"

He appeared stunned for just a moment. "Um. Okay. I'll make her a pallet."

What was that about? Lauren had the unsettling feeling that he didn't want to be alone with her. She didn't especially want to be alone with him, either. Maybe that was just her projecting her own reservations onto him. But they were going to have to coexist for a little while, in spite of how uncomfortable they made each other. It would benefit them both to learn to get along.

Lauren had never felt comfortable around strangers, and men were even more of a complication for her. Since her stepfather had never played much of an active role in her life, she had been a little slow at picking up on communication skills with the opposite sex. Her late husband had often made her feel inferior about it. She later realized that he hadn't been all that good at communication himself. But that hadn't improved her confidence any, regardless.

And the fact that Grayson was handsome enough to make any girl's heart quicken complicated matters.

She followed Grayson into the living room and watched him stretch blankets out into a square pallet. He smoothed it carefully, checking to see that it was cushiony enough. It was sweet how much care he was taking, and she wondered if he even knew he was doing it.

"Will this be okay?" He looked up at her from where he was kneeling beside the blankets.

"Of course. It's perfect." She knelt beside him, but he reached for Lily. The baby grunted slightly as her weight shifted.

Grayson situated her carefully on the little bed he had made, and Lauren couldn't help but notice how tiny the baby looked in his large hands. Lily was swaddled in a thin blanket Lauren had brought from the hospital, and Grayson tucked it in on the edge gently. Lily gave a little sigh.

"Shall we eat? I'm ready for some real food." Lauren rose from the floor and waited for him.

Grayson looked at the sleeping baby for a moment longer. "It just doesn't make sense, does it?"

She cocked her head sideways. "What doesn't?"

"Risking the life of a baby like this. She's so helpless." Something a little angry—fierce, even—took over his expression.

"Yes. It's hard to understand how Savannah could do it. I would have done everything possible to make sure Lily was protected in case something happened to me, had I been in Savannah's situation." Lauren spoke softly, and not only because of the sleeping baby. "But I'm sure she must've had her reasons. Reasons I know nothing about, or she wouldn't have been in such a situation to begin with."

He gave her an odd look as he stood. "Yeah. They always do. But that doesn't help Lily."

Grayson really didn't understand why Lauren was defending Lily's mother, but it made him feel a little guilty, and he didn't like it.

Yeah, maybe Savannah Reid had things going on he didn't know about or understand, but if he considered that, he might have to weigh the reasons other people made some of the choices they did. Like his own mother, for instance. If he considered any other reasons, things might not be as black-and-white anymore. In his career, things had to be clear-cut and right or wrong.

"Is everything okay?" Lauren's gentle question brought him back to the current situation.

"Yeah. Yeah, fine. Let's go eat." He didn't quite look her in the eye as they made their way to the kitchen.

Grayson had set the small table beside the window with simple place settings, and he motioned for her to sit. She did, and he brought the creamy pasta to the table.

They ate without a lot of conversation, and when they were almost finished their meal, Grayson noticed Lauren staring out the window into the trees.

"What are you looking at?" He asked the question casually, but her expression pushed him to reconsider the nonchalance. He followed her gaze.

"Um…hopefully nothing." She had paled a bit and continued to stare out the window. "I thought something moved over in those trees."

About the same moment she finished the words, he saw the shadow.

"Lock the door and stay close to Lily." Grayson was already moving.

His hand was on his Glock before he hit the

back door. He was sprinting by the time his feet hit the threshold. "Don't move!" He called out the words before he made the edge of the lawn.

He heard the crack of gunfire but still headed toward the shadow in the trees. He crouched slightly and began to return fire. The fact that the shadow was moving had Grayson wondering if he was trying to draw him away. He would need to proceed with caution in case this guy wasn't working alone.

He broke into the tree line and had to slow down when the heavy brush began to pull at his ankles. "Hey! I said stop!"

The shadowed figure was still moving away from him, but either Grayson had gotten a good head start on the guy or the guy was really slow. He could make out a short, stocky figure shifting through the trees.

Grayson fired again, throwing up some dirt and leaves near the man's feet. The guy let out a yelp and ran faster—as much as the crippling brush along the ground would allow, anyway. There was no path, just roots, brush and vines combined in a tangle of ground cover.

It wasn't long before Grayson lost the man in the heavy trees. He kept on for a little ways in the direction he had last seen the guy, but when the adrenaline began to subside, he realized that Lauren and Lily were vulnerable without him. Admitting defeat, he turned back.

Lauren was waiting at the door, her expression anxious.

"What are you doing out here? You should be inside with Lily." He sounded gruff, even to his own ears.

She held up one hand and showed him the video monitor picture of Lily sleeping in the living room. "She's fine. Just right behind me. What did you find?"

He blew out a frustrated breath. "Nothing. I didn't get close enough to the guy to learn anything other than he was stocky and on the small side."

"Not much to go on." She shook her head. "Another hired gun?"

"No doubt. The kidnapper's going to try anything before coming for the baby himself." He held the door for her to go back inside.

"But they know where we are. Will we be safe?" Lauren's forehead scrunched a little in concern.

"As safe as we have been so far. I have backup on the way." He hoped that might reassure her. "We can post someone on watch when they arrive."

Honestly, he would be glad when the others arrived. Cane had taken care of that little detail for him on the drive out here, as well. He had requested someone be assigned to the team who had experience with babies, hoping to give Lauren a little help because he didn't have much to offer.

They checked on Lily, and Lauren did her best to make things comfortable with Grayson, though he wished she would leave the silence alone for a while instead of trying to fill it with chatter. She tried once or twice to offer her appreciation for dinner and his help with caring for the baby, but Grayson only responded with a polite reply. His thoughts were elsewhere. Soon Lily began to demand attention with her mewling newborn cries. He was glad for the temporary diversion but found he and Lauren were far too alone for comfort again.

He tried to keep himself distracted by having Lauren show him how to change a diaper, so he could help her more. But he felt like his hands were too big, too clumsy, with such a tiny baby. Warming bottles was about the only childcare skill he seemed to have acquired.

They returned to the kitchen to clean up once Lily was settled, and Lauren tried again for conversation. This time he decided he should probably humor her.

"The pasta was delicious. Thank you for making it for us. Where did you learn to cook so well?" Lauren posed the question as she rinsed a plate in the sink.

"It was just me, my dad and my brothers. We all learned to cook." He left it at that, hoping she wouldn't question him further. He didn't like talking about the reasons his mom hadn't been around.

"Oh. Well, I never learned to cook anything fancier than a frozen pizza. I kinda wish I had, now that I'm on my own." She looked down at the sink.

"You don't have a roommate? No boyfriend to cook dinner for you?" He meant it teasingly, but when she swallowed hard and frowned, he realized his mistake.

"No. It's just me." She said no more, so he let it go for now.

They worked in silence for a few more minutes before she brought up Savannah Reid. "Do you think she has been kidnapped by the same people who are after Lily? Why would they want to take Savannah?"

Grayson pondered her question a moment before he replied. "No. I don't know what to think just yet."

"Do you think she's being held for ransom, like they planned to do with Lily?" Her rapid-fire questioning took a different turn than his thoughts.

"It's a good possibility. There is another team of marshals looking for her, though. They will find her soon." Grayson's hand went to his chest in the unconscious gesture.

"I hope you're right. It's sickening to think that

Romine might use his own child in such a manner." Lauren looked disgusted at the prospect. "But what about the marshal who was attacked?"

Grayson pressed his lips together. "I heard he was fine, but I'm still not sure how Romine got the drop on him."

"Me, either. We have good security at the hospital. It's odd." Lily began to fuss from her pallet and Lauren turned to go check on her. She paused, though, and spun around to give Grayson a questioning look. "Do you think she'll go back to sleep?"

Grayson winced and shrugged. "How should I know?" Then he glanced in the direction of the crying baby. "I'll get her."

"Are you sure?" She couldn't hide her surprise.

"I think I can manage for a moment." He gave her a crooked grin before going to the living room to retrieve the infant.

When he returned, he found Lauren watching him with concern. "Did you check to see if she's wet?"

He nodded. "Her diaper is dry, but she feels a little cold." He clasped a tiny hand. "She had kicked out of her blankets."

"She's pretty strong. I'll wrap her more tightly." She reached for Lily.

He motioned her away with his head, having the

baby carefully cradled in his arms. "She's fine for now." She felt so tiny bundled into a little cocoon of blankets, and he felt clumsy and overlarge. But his naturally protective nature welled up with a new strength at the thought.

She needed him.

"When do you expect your colleagues to arrive?" Lauren's tone was light, but she seemed anxious about the frequent silences. It made him wonder just what it was about him that made her so nervous. She seemed like a competent and confident individual otherwise.

"I expect they won't be longer than another hour or two. Then you should be able to get some rest." He adjusted his hold on the baby, who had calmed considerably with his closeness. It gave him a warm, unfamiliar feeling. This was more than the protectiveness he'd expected to feel. It was breathtaking in its tenderness.

"I'm making it okay, after the nap in the vehicle." She put away the last of the dishes and looked at the baby. "I'm more concerned about you."

"I'm used to resting at odd times when I'm on the job. I can make it as long as I need to." He meant to sound confident, but it came out sounding a little cocky.

She arched an eyebrow. "The human body has its limits, even when trained for prolonged periods of alertness. You will function better with some rest."

Ah, yes. Her scientific, trained-nurse side. He smiled.

"Oh, I'm sure that's true for most people. But when you work in law enforcement, you adapt."

She didn't argue further but shook her head. He wanted to laugh at her disapproving frown. "What? You don't believe the human body can learn to adapt for things like that?"

She cleared her throat. "I believe it can adapt. But, as with any other human ability, adaptation has its limits."

"Of course it has limits, but it also continues to gradually adapt over time." Now he was just enjoying her indignant responses.

"You're laughing at me?" If Lauren's expression was any indication, he was about to get an earful.

The moment was broken when the crunching of gravel called their attention to the driveway.

"Are those your friends?" Lauren inclined her head toward the window where they could see two plainclothes officers getting out of an SUV almost identical to the one they had arrived in.

"Friends? I really don't even know them that well. 'Colleagues' would be a more appropriate term. I've only been around them once or twice." He strode to the door, cradling Lily close.

He sensed her presence behind him. He wondered what she would think about the marshals about to join them. From what he remembered, Cole Reynolds was a rigid, by-the-book kind of guy. The total opposite of Shayla McKenzie. She was a sunbeam next to his thundercloud. The pair would make Grayson seem downright normal.

The unlikely duo approached the porch as Grayson opened the door. Shayla practically bounced up the walk in her aviators, while Cole's dark scowl accompanied him all the way to the door.

"Marshal Thorpe." Cole didn't do much more than nod as he brushed past them into the house. He barely glanced at the child.

Shayla, on the other hand, stopped to pull off her sunglasses and extend a hand. "Great to see you again, Thorpe."

He took her hand and returned her greeting before watching her turn to Lauren. "Hi, I'm Shayla McKenzie. I assume you're Miss Beck?"

Lauren looked thunderstruck in the wake of the odd pair. "You can call me Lauren."

"Great to meet you, Lauren." She turned back to Lily, nestled in Grayson's arms. "And this little sweet thing?"

"This is Lily," Grayson said. "The innocent victim in all of this."

"Hello, Miss Lily. You're such a beauty! Mind if I hold her?" Without preamble, she took the child from his arms.

Before he knew what was happening, the two women launched into a conversation about the baby that had his head spinning. He made his excuses and went to find Cole.

"You got here fast." Grayson dropped down into the chair across from where Cole was setting up his laptop.

"You would, too, if you were stuck in the car with McKenzie." Not a hint of amusement colored Cole's tone.

Nevertheless, Grayson chuckled. "She can't be that bad."

Cole looked up with a disbelieving frown, one brow cocked. "No. She's worse."

Grayson sobered. "You'd better get used to her. We could all be stuck here together for a while."

He hadn't believed Cole's expression could get much darker, but it did. "What do you mean? This should be a pretty cut-and-dried case. It's likely Romine who is after the baby. You've been studying his case. So we just apprehend him and send the baby back to her mother. It's likely he's hiding out at his brother's ranch in Texas. There is a team on the way there as we speak."

"Yes." Grayson stacked his fingers together. "But it might not be as simple as all that."

"What do you mean?" Cole straightened and focused on Grayson.

"We need to find Savannah Reid. I think Romine plans to attempt to get money from her father, Senator Reid. There's a possibility Romine will harm her if Reid doesn't cooperate. And aside from that, with the senator as powerful as he is, it's quite possible Romine isn't the one trying to abduct the baby."

"Excuse me?" Cole's expression indicated he'd never considered such a possibility.

"The mother was kidnapped from the hospital about the time a man tried to abduct the baby. The security guard at the hospital said it looked like there was a struggle in her room. The marshal protecting her was hit over the head, tied up and stuffed in a closet. If it was Romine or one of his men who tried to take the baby, it's possible he took Savannah at the same time." A knot formed in the pit of Grayson's stomach.

Cole spoke his thoughts aloud. "It's a sick man who would use his own child to get ransom money from his daughter's grandfather."

"I agree. But Romine knows we are close to getting him, and he will do anything to get out of the country right now. If the child is truly his, maybe he won't harm her. But that's more than I can say for the child's mother. And I'm not sure I trust Senator Reid, which complicates things even more. That means we have twice the number of twisted minds to deal with." Grayson sat back in the chair. "I can tell you, I have my doubts about

Senator Reid's integrity. But I don't think he would kidnap his own blood to try to extort money."

The sound of women's voices warned them of their approach. Cole inclined his head. "The nurse. What does she know?"

"Pretty much all we do, right now."

Cole nodded. "How's she handling it?"

"As well as you'd expect, I guess. I think she's tougher than she seems, though." He thought about Lauren's staunch defense of the baby in the face of the men who had tried to kidnap Lily. She was pure steel when she was sticking up for someone else.

Shayla stuck her head in the door of the room Cole had set up as a temporary office. "Can we crash your party?"

Her smile was infectious. Grayson noticed it only served to deepen Cole's scowl, however. "Nothing to crash. Just talking business."

Lauren wasn't exactly smiling, but he noticed that the lines of tension had relaxed around her mouth as she followed Shayla into the room.

"Lauren says the senator's daughter has also been kidnapped." Shayla cut to the chase, almost as if she already knew what the men had been discussing. Had she overheard them, or was it just a coincidence?

"And Shayla tells me that you might have information as to Romine's whereabouts right now," Lauren added.

Grayson looked over at Lauren. "You two seem to have covered a lot of information pretty quickly."

"Is there some reason I shouldn't know what is going on?" Lauren looked a little injured.

"No, I don't suppose there is. I just didn't think you were…" He hesitated. Of course she was interested. She was up to her ears in this situation whether he liked it or not. Why hadn't he told her more about what he knew?

"I know I'm not a marshal like the rest of you, and maybe you have to keep some things confidential. But maybe I can help." As soon as she said it, her face turned pink. Why was she embarrassed? She didn't have any reason to be.

"I didn't mean to leave you out, Lauren. I guess I wasn't thinking about it. I get absorbed in my job sometimes." He tried for a conciliatory tone, hoping she didn't take it as patronizing.

She smiled, but it seemed a little forced. "It's okay. I'm going to go check on Lily."

Lauren fled to her room. She was so far out of her comfort zone. She wished she could take back her words. She didn't know anything at all about the work the marshals were doing. They probably thought she was really silly. She hadn't made the impression she would have liked to make on these people she didn't know. She barely knew Grayson, if the truth were told.

Taking deep breaths and trying to think of other things, she worked through it. She had relaxed a little when Shayla had arrived, finally feeling like maybe she could talk to someone who might understand, because Grayson didn't want to share details with her. But maybe she had made a mistake. She had no business being so deeply involved in this situation. Why did this have to happen on her shift? If it hadn't, maybe she wouldn't be here now, feeling like she was the outsider. She needed to focus on Lily, not feel sorry for herself. Ridiculous.

The worst part was that it frightened her in a new way thinking that maybe Grayson hadn't told her things about the case for a reason. It brought back too many thoughts of Marcus, her former husband, and how he had wanted to control everything she did—who she talked to, what she said, where she went, even what clothing she wore. He had kept things from her all the time. When she'd found out, he'd claimed that her shortcomings had kept him from telling her. She had nearly suffocated under his constant pushing and demands. Nothing she did without his prior approval had ever been right or okay. It had gotten to the point he'd been very nearly violent, raising a hand to her one day over something she'd said.

She'd known then it was time to get out of the relationship. Before she could ask for a divorce, though, he had been killed in a freak accident. She had never wanted another relationship since. At least as a single person she was free to be herself.

Lauren heard the footsteps coming down the hall, but she didn't move, thinking it was probably Shayla. The knock at the door came an instant later.

"I'll be out in a minute." She tried to keep her tone light. She didn't want to talk about the reasons she was upset just yet.

It surprised her when Grayson's voice came through the door. "Uh, Lauren, I know I upset you. Can I talk to you for a minute?"

She didn't really know what to say. "I'm fine. We can talk later."

She thought she heard him sigh. "Will you please open the door?"

Something in his tone changed her mind. She paused a moment before answering. She couldn't refuse him. "Okay."

She rose from the bed and walked over to open the door. His contrite little-boy expression softened her just a bit more. "What is it?"

"I just want to apologize for making you feel like you were in the dark. I really thought that maybe the less you knew, the better it would be for you if we were to become separated or something. I see now that wasn't fair. Forgive me?" He stuck out a hand. She looked at it in amusement.

"It's okay. It's possible I might have overreacted a bit." She took his offered hand, feeling silly until his touch sparked an electrical reaction in her. She jerked her hand back.

He looked down at his hand, as if he, too, felt a little confused. "No, you didn't. You have every right to know what is happening, and I need to remember that. I shouldn't be so insensitive.

"We just learned that Romine has contacted Senator Reid, asking for ransom money for his daughter's safe return. The senator is reluctant to comply, considering the circumstances. We feel that's why they've become so aggressive with trying to get Lily, as well." Grayson's voice was level but concerned.

He finally looked up from his hand and straight into her eyes. Tenderness shone in his blue eyes, and her heart gave a little thud. Uh-oh. Good thing this was a temporary arrangement.

"I'm sure you aren't accustomed to people being so nosy." She gave a little laugh. "It probably seems silly to you. You deal with this stuff every day."

"You aren't nosy or silly." He paused a moment. "You're smart, and having your help will be a privilege."

"I haven't had a lot of time to be anything else." She smiled to soften the statement.

"Lauren, I know it probably isn't any of my business, but what happened to make you so wary of me? You don't seem to want to trust me. Did someone hurt you?" He looked afraid of the answer.

"No. Not like that, anyway. I was married." She paused to look him in the eye. "He—died. But I had already been to see a lawyer. He was very, um, controlling. He didn't want me to have a life of my own. Everything had to revolve around him."

Grayson frowned. "I promise if I ask you to do something, it will be for your protection. I might not always have time to explain, under the circumstances, but you can trust me."

She nodded. "You've never been married?"

His expression turned fierce. "No. My parents had a rocky marriage. I had a close call once, but Rebecca also proved to be a bad idea. She wasn't who I thought she was. I haven't dated since we broke off our engagement."

"Ouch. I guess you're glad you found out before the wedding, though."

She watched as he hesitated. She couldn't help wondering if he was trying to decide how much to tell her. "Yes, I was glad things turned out the way they did. She betrayed me, but I managed to salvage the situation before anyone was seriously injured."

Lauren reached for his arm. "What do you mean?"

When he raised his eyes, they were full of anguish. It made Lauren regret asking the question, but her curiosity had gotten the better of her. She was about to tell him he didn't have to talk about it when he spoke again.

"She was an informant. A spy. And I fell for her act. She had everyone believing her innocent kindergarten-teacher act. A bunch of local church ladies thought it would be cute to get us together."

He paused for so long, Lauren thought he might not go on. He finally did. "She almost got my whole team killed on a mission to bust a drug house because she had told them we were coming. We got to the decrepit old house, and I knew something was wrong. The usual signs of a bust were off. It smelled like cigarettes, and all I could think of was the way Rebecca had always tried to sneak around and smoke, even though she knew I didn't like it. That was the last thing I remembered thinking before everything went south. They were waiting on us with AK-47s."

Lauren was shocked into silence for a moment. "She set a trap for you?"

His eyes took on a troubled look. "Yes. We almost didn't get out without losing everyone on the team. Four guys were seriously injured."

"Including you?"

"Yeah. Including me. By the time I got out of the hospital, she had her act all planned out. She tried to make it sound like she had been forced into it. I didn't have enough on her to throw her in jail." Was he wondering how he would have felt if she had gone to prison?

"So you just broke things off with her, and she went free?"

Grayson nodded. "There was nothing else I could do. She's out there somewhere, though, free to pull the same stunt on another unsuspecting man. I never saw it coming."

His anguish was apparent in every word, so she tried to soothe him. "It's okay. You had no way of knowing you couldn't trust her."

"No, it wasn't okay. It's my job to know. I could have gotten us all killed."

"Well, no lasting harm was done, though, right? Everyone recovered?"

"Yeah. Everyone survived, but it was a lesson learned."

She only hesitated a moment before embracing him. To her surprise, he allowed it.

"I turned to God after that. I knew then I couldn't forgive myself on my own. I could only do so in Him."

Lauren wanted to sob for him, but she managed to hold it in and stay strong. "I'm so glad you did, Grayson."

"To this day, I can't stand the smell of cigarettes." He squeezed her to him, and she felt relief, along with some tender emotion she couldn't name, just knowing he had shared something so personal with her. His story tugged at her heart.

And it made him that much more of a hero in her eyes.

Grayson had left with Cole to check the status of the case not long after that. She was still mulling over his story—and how much it explained—when he returned with news.

"I thought you'd want to know I have an update on the external workings of the case."

"Oh? What is that?" Lauren was interested but a bit distracted from their prior conversation.

"We had a team sent out to Romine's brother's ranch, but they found the place deserted. But the research Cole has been doing nonstop to avoid Shayla is paying off. It seems that while Savannah Reid hasn't been in any trouble herself, she has a friend whom she has helped evade several charges—including drug ones—against her. That particular friend happens to live in Texas, just a short drive from Romine's ranch. We think she may be involved." Grayson frowned.

"Do you think that's where they have taken Savannah?" Lauren pressed, even though she already suspected this was the case. She nodded, her eyes searching his face.

"It's a good possibility. We're working on finding a link between Savannah's friend and Romine, as well." Grayson started to leave. "We're trying to get this over with as soon as possible."

"I appreciate that. I'd like to get back to my normal life sooner rather than later." Lauren gave a little laugh, but it held no humor. Really, though, she was beginning to think this wasn't so bad. Taking care of Lily was a joy, Shayla was making her more comfortable, and Grayson was growing on her.

Grayson nodded. "I know you would. It shouldn't be too long."

But the hours were creeping by, and Lauren knew it wasn't going to get any better until the kidnapper was caught.

SIX

Lily's cries awakened Lauren in the middle of the night. Rising from the warm bed, Lauren gathered the baby next to her as she headed for the kitchen to warm a bottle. At first, she was groggy and just wanted to take care of Lily's 1:00 a.m. feeding, but when she walked through the living room on the way to the kitchen, she saw a shadow move outside the window.

Sucking in a breath, she clutched Lily close and turned to sprint back up the stairs to wake Grayson. But before she could launch in that direction, a strong hand grabbed her by the arm. A squeak was out before he was able to quiet her. She let out a sigh. He must have heard her get up and followed her downstairs.

"You scared me, Grayson," she said in a loud whisper. He turned toward her with a finger to his lips just as glass shattering in the living room set off the alarm.

He had released her and pulled his Glock before

Lauren could even react. "Get the baby out of here. She's too exposed in the living room with all these windows. Take her to Shayla's bedroom. Hurry."

Her body began to move even before her mind could fully comprehend what was happening. Her arms tightened around Lily while she tried to process where she was going. Even as she debated, Cole and Shayla appeared from their corners of the house. Shayla took charge, hustling Lauren and the baby into a small closet.

"I'm sorry. It's going to be tight, but I'll be right here to let you out as soon as the threat is neutralized." Shayla's words were reassuring, the lilt of her voice belying her fiercely defensive stance. "We don't have time to find a better hiding place."

Lauren clutched Lily to her chest, wishing she had something more than the pacifier to soothe the baby. It was unlikely that it would satisfy the child for long, and if the objective was to keep their location secret, Lily's unhappy cries would be sure to give them away.

The sounds coming from outside the closet held no reassurance for her, either. Shouting and scuffing ensued for what seemed like far too long. Lily fussed a bit, and Lauren did her best to rock her and encourage her to take the pacifier. She just knew they were about to be discovered.

Finally, things went still, and Lauren could hear Cole saying that he had the intruder secured. A few minutes passed and she could only assume the marshals were clearing the property to ensure there was no other threat. She didn't like the way she was beginning to feel at being closed up. The air was heavy, too dense. The intense darkness pressed around her, and her nerve endings seemed hypersensitive. Her hold on the baby felt like more than she could maintain. Her breathing quickened. She closed her eyes and tried to focus on slowing down her breaths.

"Lauren, are you okay?"

She hadn't realized the door had opened and Grayson was standing there, scrutinizing her. An instantaneous heat flooded her cheeks. The man always seemed to catch her at her worst.

"Yes. Just ready to get out of here." She tried to push past him with the remarkably calm baby.

"Are you claustrophobic?" His curious expression was charming.

"No. I mean, yes. I mean— Well… I didn't think so, but I guess I am." Her pulse was still pounding, and his close scrutiny wasn't helping.

His lips curled to one side in an expression that wasn't quite a smile, but also wasn't his normal, flat countenance.

Lily intervened at last, drawing their attention with a sudden outburst.

Grayson winced. "Well, I guess being locked

in a closet is one way to find out. I sent Shayla to get a bottle ready for the baby."

"Thanks." Lauren shifted the tiny bundle in her arms and Grayson reached for her.

"Let me take her. You look a little pale."

Lauren allowed him to take Lily, rubbing her over-sensitized arms as soon as they were free. She breathed fresh air deeply into her lungs, letting her eyelids close once more for a second.

"Go back to bed. We can handle Lily." Grayson sounded a bit curt and her eyes popped open in surprise.

"I'm fine. I mean, I will be in just a second. Besides, I doubt I could sleep." She didn't want to abandon Lily right now. Even though she knew Shayla was perfectly capable with the baby, Lauren wanted to keep her close. The possibility of someone taking her was now just too real to let the infant out of her sight.

A thought occurred to her then. "What happened to the intruder?" She hadn't heard anyone leave, but she also hadn't seen Cole.

"Cole took him to the basement for questioning. It's quieter with fewer distractions down there." Grayson started walking toward the kitchen, presumably to check on Shayla's progress with the bottle.

"He doesn't care for crying babies, huh?" Lauren found that thought amusing. Boy, had he landed in the wrong assignment.

"I think it was more about avoiding Shayla." There was amusement in his tone, as well.

Lauren giggled. "What's the deal with that?"

"He doesn't know how to handle her. He calls her Little Miss Sunshine." Grayson had stopped walking, probably so that Shayla wouldn't over-hear their conversation.

"She isn't that bad!" Lauren burst out laughing.

"No, but Cole can be Mr. Doom and Gloom himself." Grayson frowned as if to emphasize his point.

Shayla appeared then, coming out of the kitchen. "Are you talking about Cole? He could make the Grim Reaper look pleasant. Someone should really get that man to lighten up."

Grayson and Lauren exchanged a glance.

"He just takes his job seriously," Grayson said.

"He takes everything seriously. *Too* seriously. He wouldn't know fun if it knocked him over the head." Shayla handed over the bottle. "Let me take the baby. You can take a breather, maybe get some tea or a snack."

Grayson grinned as Shayla turned to him. "You're leaving it to me to help Cole with the in-terrogation? Don't you want to do it?"

"Cole wouldn't welcome my interference."

She rolled her eyes before focusing her attention on Lily.

"Exactly. So where's the fun in that?" Grayson reached for Lily. "Don't cut him any breaks."

Shayla sighed, snuggling Lily before handing her over. "Fine. You get to have all the fun."

But her wink said she was going to enjoy annoying Cole just as much.

The man who had broken into the house sat rigidly in a straight-backed chair facing Cole. He was big and burly in every sense of the word. His chest muscles bulged beneath his shirt, his secured arms pushing them forward because his hands were cuffed behind his back. He wasn't looking at Cole, but his expression was nothing short of mean.

Grayson expected to hear an occasional growl coming from something so angry-looking. He hadn't expected the hired man to be so sullen.

Since Lauren held the now sleeping Lily, Grayson made sure she was settled out of the way where he could keep an eye on them both, but the man they were questioning didn't have a good view of them.

"Things will go a lot easier on you if you'll just talk." Cole looked almost as angry as the bear of a man avoiding eye contact with him from the chair.

The man didn't speak, didn't even look at him.

When Grayson approached, Cole looked his way.

"Nothing?" Grayson ventured, his brow creasing.

"Not a word." Cole shook his head. "Might as well be mute."

Grayson picked up the wallet they had found on the man and a photo fell out while he looked at the man's ID. A woman and small child stared up at him. Grayson picked it up.

"Jonathan Paretti. Native of Texas." He held up the photo with two fingers. "Your wife and child?"

The man dared a glance in his direction, his expression altering slightly. Was that a flicker of concern? He still didn't speak.

Shayla nodded and picked up the questioning.

"I'm sure they need you at home. You probably took this job because Romine offered you a lot of money, and no doubt you wanted to make a better life for them." She paused. The man wasn't looking at anyone, but judging by Paretti's expression, he could hear everything just fine.

Lauren listened intently. When Paretti looked her way, Grayson tensed, wondering if he had misjudged her position out of eyesight. He moved to where the guy sat and double-checked. Relief filled him when he was sure the guy couldn't see them. He knew Paretti wasn't a threat now that he was in custody, but he didn't like thinking he might know anything about Lauren, just the same.

Cole chimed in. "I'm sure it didn't feel like you were doing anything wrong, since the child is Romine's daughter. He probably told you we were holding her hostage to try to get to him, or something like that."

Grayson nodded. "It's sad to have to protect a child from her father. But he seems to think her grandfather will give up some cash to save her life. We just got word that he is trying to ransom the senator's daughter. Probably plans to use the baby if that doesn't work. That just goes to show you that the man has no loyalty to anyone but himself. This is his own flesh and blood we're talking about here."

He could see the thoughts churning in the man's head. Paretti's eyes widened.

"Now, I don't know..." Cole picked up the dialogue. "Maybe you've worked for Romine before. If so, I hope he compensated you well, because our people are currently looking into your record. But if you are refusing to talk out of loyalty to Romine, I hope you realize he wouldn't do the same for you. I have heard that he turned on his own brother. So if you're thinking it's just the kid... well, I wouldn't count on it."

Grayson stepped toward him. "If you want to make sure your wife and kid don't pay the price when Romine finds out you've failed, you'd better start talking fast. We can only protect them if you help us out."

For a second, he thought the man would still refuse to talk. But then his gaze landed on the family photo that Grayson still held in his hand. "I'll talk. Just keep my family safe."

Cole almost smiled. "Good. Where do we find Romine?"

"I—I don't know anything about Romine. The guy who hired me gave me a burner phone he uses to contact me. I have no way to contact him. I've never met Arnie Romine. I don't even know if it's him." Paretti frowned.

"Okay, then. Where were you supposed to take the baby if you succeeded?" Grayson put a hand on one hip.

"Uh, just to a gas station outside town. Then someone was supposed to meet me and take her off my hands." He shrugged.

"How were you supposed to know who to give her to?" Grayson checked to see that Cole, ever the meticulous one, was getting it all down. He was.

"She was going to say 'It's a nice night for a drive,' and I would say 'I love the lake this time of year' so she would know it was me. Then we were to switch vehicles with the baby inside. The rest of my money would come through after they got the kid and I returned the vehicle to the rental lot." Paretti looked annoyed now. No telling how much money he had been promised.

"So it was a woman you were supposed to meet?" Cole asked. "Did she know what you look like?"

"No. Neither of us was given any further information. The gas station is secluded and not busy this time of night." He shrugged one massive shoulder. "I guess he thought we wouldn't run into anyone else."

Cole and Grayson exchanged a glance. "Is there a way the man who hired you would know if you were captured?" Cole asked.

"Only if I didn't show up."

Grayson nodded at Cole. "Perfect. Where's your car?"

"It's in the woods, up the hill on a side road. Hey, what are you gonna do? What about my family?" His face was turning red.

"Calm down, Mr. Paretti. We're taking care of it." Cole rose to conclude the questioning. "You can give your information to Marshal Thorpe here, and he will send out protection. Meanwhile, I'm going to get you some insurance that nothing happens to them before he gets the chance."

Cole strode out of the room, and Paretti began to calm a little as Grayson verified the address on his ID, then took down everything he could tell him about his family that might help keep them

safe. When he had finished, Grayson called headquarters and dispatched a team to Paretti's home to
provide protection for the man's wife and daughter.

"Hey, Marshal, can I give her a call? She will
be scared if I don't talk to her. Let me call my
wife." Concern filled the man's eyes. He didn't
look nearly as mean now.

Compassion flooded Grayson. It was risky.
What if the man didn't do what he said he would?
What if he called someone else? He could be lying
about not knowing how to contact Romine. Or
they could have an emergency plan in place in
case he was captured.

Grayson looked the guy over, seeing not the
hired thug who'd tried to kidnap a child for money,
but the desperate man who wanted to provide for
his family. Yet it went against all the wisdom he
possessed. Even something as simple as the man
calling his wife could be some sort of signal that
things had gone awry. He couldn't risk it.

"I'm sorry. I'll let you call her as soon as this
is all taken care of. But I can't take the risk of allowing you to make a phone call right now. There
are too many lives at stake." Grayson didn't have
to try to sound sympathetic. He wished he could
trust the guy.

"Will I be released? Or am I going to jail?" Paretti sounded tired now.

"I'll have to take you in for further questioning,

but we will get you a good deal." Grayson didn't say any more. All they really had on the guy was breaking and entering, even though they knew he'd been after the baby. He hadn't gotten to her, thanks to Lauren and Shayla's quick thinking.

Cole returned with Shayla on his heels. "Let's go, Thorpe. I'll explain on the way."

Grayson nodded. He turned to Lauren briefly. "Shayla will make sure you and Lily are safe until we return."

Cole actually smiled as they left, leading the way as Grayson carried the "baby," which was actually a sack of flour bundled up to look like the child.

"Are you losing it, man? You're smiling." Grayson shook his head. "We could be walking into a trap."

"I'm smiling because we're leaving that bum to have to listen to Little Miss Sunshine until we get back. Serves him right." He chuckled—actually *chuckled*. Grayson had never heard anything faintly resembling mirth come from the man.

Grayson was still shaking his head. "Yep. You've lost it."

"Nope. Just glad to be getting out of that house. And she's bound to annoy Paretti." Cole was practically skipping.

"Dude. Shayla really isn't that bad. She doesn't

annoy anyone but you. I think you have another problem with her." Grayson laughed.

Cole froze. "Like what?"

Grayson gave him a little shove to get him moving again. "That you *like* her."

"Don't be ridiculous. She drives me crazy." He almost snarled the words.

"Exactly."

Cole looked shell-shocked. He shook his head and picked up his pace. "That's stupid."

But his voice didn't hold nearly as much conviction as before.

Lauren felt completely alone, even though Grayson and Cole had sent in extra men from the Marshals Service for protection while they were gone. They had been on duty out along the road to the house, watching since just after Paretti had shown up. He couldn't have planned his breach any better, it seemed.

Shayla was downstairs babysitting him in case he decided to share any more information or try anything stupid. The new guys weren't exactly the social type. Lily was sleeping, and though it was still in the wee hours of the morning, Lauren was wide-awake. She was worried for Grayson's safety, and that concerned her, as well.

Sure, it was normal to want someone to be safe, but the knot of anxiety in her stomach didn't indicate a typical level of concern. She kept thinking about all the things that could go wrong. What if it was a trap? What if the kidnapper had it all planned out and decided to kill them if they showed up in place of his hired man without the baby? He could be watching, and he would know who Grayson was. So many scenarios played in her head. So many things could happen.

Trying to distract herself, she turned on the TV. The local news was on, and coincidentally, the reporter was talking about Arnie Romine. Interested, she paused and listened to the report.

"Some say Romine's organization has been a rival of the Harmon gang for decades, but we have no confirmation of that story at this time. We do, however, know that three members of the Harmon gang have been shot. Two are dead, while one is in critical condition. Only one man associated with Romine has been reported injured, but onlookers say they believe one other man was dragged into a nearby vehicle with possible injuries, as well. Some onlookers say that there have been threats about a possible war escalating between the two gangs.

"A source says Harmon may be after Arnold Romine's alleged child. Other sources say the gangs have reached an agreement. Local police are investigating the matter at this time." The pretty reporter nodded at the camera and sent the transmission back to the studio reporters, but not before Lauren got a glimpse of a nice neighborhood strewn with crime scene tape in the background. A black Cadillac Escalade riddled with bullet holes sitting along the curb not far behind the reporter illustrated the severity of what had happened there.

These were the kinds of people who wanted Lily… This was the kind of danger such an innocent child was in.

Lauren turned off the television and walked over to the sleeping baby. Looking down at the innocent face, she allowed all her bottled-up tears to release. She just stood there crying for several minutes, letting the tears cleanse her—body and soul. But when they stopped, she took a deep, almost violent breath. It was time to toughen up. She was going to protect this child if she was the only one who could. She would do whatever she had to do to keep Lily safe.

She would either keep her safe or die trying.

She went to find Shayla as soon as she was assured that Lily's monitor was working well. She only intended to be gone a moment, anyway.

Shayla met her on the stairs. "Oh, Lauren. I was just coming to check on you and Lily. Is she sleeping?"

At Lauren's nod, disappointment came over Shayla's face.

"I will let you know when she wakes, and if you aren't busy, you can hold her then." Lauren smiled at her. "But I wanted to talk to you about something I just saw on the news. It might affect Lily's safety."

"What is it?" Shayla turned her head sideways in question.

"Do you know anything about the Harmon gang and their rivalry with Romine's?"

"Just that there is one. What does that have to do with Lily?" Shayla looked confused.

"The reporter said that a war is escalating between the two gangs and that Harmon's gang might be after Lily. They called her his 'alleged child,' but I'm sure it was her they referred to." Lauren was shaking. She was so afraid for Lily. If she was Romine's daughter, he at least wouldn't harm her, but this rival gang… That was a whole other story. They might do anything to get to Romine.

Shayla had paled, as well. "Maybe the reports are false." But she put a hand to her head. "How did they find out about Lily? No one except the parents, a few marshals and a handful of hospital staff is supposed to know anything about her. They have been asked to keep it quiet. Someone is talking. And something isn't right."

"Somehow they have found us everywhere we

go with Lily. How could that be?" Lauren was afraid to voice what she feared.

Shayla did. "I have to call Grayson. I think we might have a leak."

Grayson had allowed Cole to drive, only because he wanted to be the one to remain in the car when they made the switch. The plan was to get the woman in the car before she knew Grayson was there. If she would take them to the next drop spot, they would be able to identify and arrest another of the kidnapper's people. The more of his cohorts they could get to cooperate with them, the closer the marshals would be to capturing the kidnapper himself. Eventually, they would hit on someone who knew where he was. If not, sooner or later, he would come after the baby himself— whoever it was behind this.

The roads wound tightly through the hills, so their pace was slower than Grayson would have liked. It was too dark to see much, but the heavy copses of trees on either side of the road made it feel closed in and shut off from the rest of the world. Clouds drifted in front of what little sliver of moon there was. The rain they had been hammered with the last few hours might still be hanging around.

"According to Paretti, the gas station should be up here on the left." Cole gripped the steering wheel of Paretti's Honda Accord. "You'd better get in place."

Grayson had to work to get his tall, muscular frame out of sight behind the driver's seat. Thankfully, Cole's legs weren't quite as long as his, so he'd moved up the seat enough to give Grayson some room. The child carrier was on the opposite side and he hoped the woman wouldn't look too closely before getting into the car. If she realized it wasn't really the baby, she might do something stupid.

The ideal situation would be to stay hidden and let her take the child to her destination, but it would be impossible for his presence to go undetected for so long. So he intended to show her his badge once she was where she couldn't flee, then have her continue with the plan. Cole would follow at a safe distance in the exchange vehicle until they reached their destination.

Grayson couldn't see much from his awkward position, so Cole spoke quietly, giving him the layout. "She's here. We are parked between the gas pumps and the road, under a dim streetlight. Her vehicle is a small crossover SUV. Looks like one of those newer Toyotas. It's dark red. It has the star-shaped sticker on the back glass that Paretti said he was to look for. There's no one else here and the station is closed. I will leave in the opposite direction, so as not to tip her off too early, and double back."

Before Grayson could have any second thoughts, Cole was getting out of the car. His thoughts went unexpectedly to Lauren. Was she safe with Carlos and Jeff, the marshals who'd taken his and Cole's covers when they'd left? Was Lily giving her any trouble? Did she get any rest at all?

As if in response to his thoughts, a text came through from Shayla.

More trouble. Harmon gang could be involved. Text back ASAP.

Would Lily and Lauren be safe until he could get back? Was Shayla prepared in case of another attempted kidnapping while he was gone?

He shook away the thoughts. It was a bad time to be having them. Of course Shayla could handle it. She was one of the most competent marshals he knew. He needed to focus. He had a job to do.

Grayson could barely make out the voices as Cole and the woman exchanged words. Then it was quiet as she opened the car door. He felt her weight shift the seat in front of him as she settled into the car. A thud and a puff of air came as she closed the door and the engine sputtered to life. Grayson steeled himself, willing every muscle in his body to remain still.

She never looked back, just sped onto the highway, throwing gravel as she went. She hit the gas with a heavy foot and took the first curve a little too quickly. The thought occurred to Grayson that whoever the kidnapper was, he clearly wasn't too concerned about the child's safety. This woman drove like a maniac.

Before Grayson could make his presence known, she was on the phone. "Yeah, I've got the package. Headed your way. I don't know. Sure, I'll check." She disconnected.

When the woman slowed to turn and check out the child, Grayson rose from his crouch behind the seat, badge at the ready, his other hand on his Glock, just in case. He spoke before she could react. "US marshal. Listen carefully. I want you to keep driving to your appointed destination. I have a gun and I will use it if you choose not to cooperate."

The woman's eyes widened before she turned to look at the road. Her breathing started coming fast. "Oh my—" She looked back at Grayson again and cursed.

He hadn't anticipated her reaction. Her calculating eyes were searching right and left. Then they gleamed. Anxiety bubbled up in him. This wasn't good. What was she going to do?

Before he could guess her intentions, she jerked the wheel, sending the car careening down a steep embankment. Grayson's head slammed against the side window. The Honda rolled several times, smashing into rocks on the way down.

Grayson, without a seat belt, tumbled heavily around the car's interior until it finally came to an abrupt rest. White powder from the now damaged bag of flour filled the air like a heavy cloud. The vehicle, leaning against a tree, was up on its side, but the woman wasted no time. The driver's door was facing the sky, but she pried it open with considerable strength for a woman her size and began to hoist herself out. Grayson waved the flour cloud out of his face as he scrambled to follow, not entirely sure nothing was broken, but not about to let her get away. He couldn't see her well through the powdery haze, but he could see enough to know she was on the run.

She hopped down and, as he'd expected, took off at a quick sprint. "Hey! Stop!"

Getting his large frame out of the car proved more difficult than Grayson had anticipated, giving him a new appreciation for the woman's strength and agility. He would have a fun time chasing her down with his banged-up frame.

He pulled his Glock, shooting at the ground near her feet, hoping to scare her into stopping. No help there. She jumped and picked up speed.

He hopped from the car and chased her into the woods, calling Cole on the run. "Hurry up, buddy. The woman pulled a crazy stunt. I'm pursuing on foot."

"Almost there," Cole reassured him. "I see where the car went off the road."

The woman was agile, but slow. Grayson's long legs quickly caught up with her, and he rolled her to the ground in one swift motion. He had cuffs on her by the time Cole came skidding down the embankment.

"I thought you needed backup?" He shot him a look of disappointment.

Grayson jerked the woman to her feet. "Nah. Just a ride home."

SEVEN

Lauren's pulse ratcheted up a few notches as the unfamiliar vehicle pulled up to the house in the early morning light. She froze by the temporarily repaired living room window, uncertain if she should make a run for Lily or call for Shayla.

Relief swept through her when she recognized Grayson's handsome face through the windshield. He had never looked better as he got out of the car to reveal scrapes and bruises along his square jaw and temple. He saw her watching him and sent her a crooked grin. Heat suffused her cheeks, but she continued to watch as he helped Cole haul a woman out of the car. She was young, maybe in her early twenties, and had thick dark hair that hung past her shoulders. She wore heavy bangs across her forehead, and attitude was written all over her face. She was pretty tiny, though, which Lauren found comical in comparison to the attitude.

Grayson followed them up the porch steps to the door, where Lauren met him.

"Grayson, are you okay?" Lauren touched his cheek and then thought better of it, pulling back.

"I'm fine. Miss Angelina Burris here thought it would be fun to thwart our plans by driving down a steep embankment to try to get away." Grayson gestured to the woman Cole was bringing into the house. Shayla was coming up the basement stairs.

"Shayla, let the boss know they'll need to pick up two today instead of one." Cole took the woman past Shayla and down the stairs to where Paretti was still being held.

"Wow. It's been a busy night." Shayla laughed. "I'll let him know."

"Where's Lily?" Grayson asked, running a hand across his forehead.

"She's sleeping. You should shower before the others leave. I can help Shayla and Cole if they need me." Lauren plucked some grass from his shirt on the back of his shoulder.

"I need one that bad, huh?"

She avoided his question. "Are you sure you aren't injured anywhere?"

"I'm good. I'll be back in ten."

Grayson strode off to the shower, not a hint of fatigue in his self-assured manner. She shook her head at his inexhaustible energy.

Lauren wanted to go down the stairs to see what was happening with the woman, but she didn't want to interrupt without permission. She didn't know if they would be okay with it. Grayson had allowed it the first time. She would just have to wait for Grayson to tell her about everything that was happening.

Shayla came up the stairs then, rolling her eyes. "Cole doesn't want to start questioning her until Grayson gets back, so here we are. I'll wait with you until he's done."

Shayla plopped her skinny frame down on the sofa, so Lauren sat in the chair across from her. "He won't be long."

"That's good, because I'm not usually good at being patient." Shayla laughed, shaking her blond head.

The two women sipped coffee and discussed some mundane things, along with rehashing what they knew about the case so far. It just felt like they were missing something that might tie it all together, but no amount of talking about it was making things any clearer. Lauren couldn't help feeling this sort of job would have some frustrating moments.

Shayla, however, seemed to love the thinking process and going through the details repetitively to try to solve the mysteries surrounding the case. Lauren found her joy was contagious.

"Are you ready to go help Cole interrogate, Shayla?" Grayson asked, entering the living room. His hair was damp, and the scent of the masculine shower gel he had used drifted into the room alongside him. Lauren tried to ignore the surge of interest that rushed through her.

Shayla rubbed her hands together. "Of course. But before we do, Lauren is going to fill you in on the details about the escalating gang war."

"Yeah, I didn't really know what to think from your text. We never quite connected on that. What exactly is going on?" Grayson looked from Shayla to Lauren and back again.

"Romine's people are warring with the Harmon gang." Shayla stood. "They shot up a neighborhood last night in Houston."

She had gained Grayson's full attention. "Really? That's terrible. Although, I can't say I'm all that surprised. If Romine is behind this, maybe it will detract some of his attention for a day or two. If he has other things to worry about, maybe he'll stop looking for the baby." Grayson frowned even as he made the hopeful statement.

"You don't believe that, though, do you." Lauren's soft voice made the assertion.

Shayla grimaced. "A man like Romine has so many resources... He probably isn't even near Houston. It could be a long time before Lily's safe—if ever."

"Yes, we need to get the WITSEC paperwork done and set her up with a new identity. She's going to need to disappear."

Lauren felt a hard knot swell in her chest. "You mean put her in witness protection? But she's not a witness. And she's just an infant. Isn't that a little unorthodox?"

Grayson shoved his hands in his back pockets. "Unorthodox, maybe, but it may be her only chance. You'd be surprised at how often it happens. Do you want her growing up in the middle of gang wars and drug-lord rivalries?"

"Absolutely not. But why not just put her up for adoption? If her mother doesn't come back for her, that is." Lauren couldn't imagine any mother choosing not to return for such a precious child. It saddened her to think of the rough start this tiny girl was getting in life.

"For one thing, Lauren, that would endanger any family that adopted her. She has to disappear, or her life will remain in danger." Grayson looked at her sympathetically.

Grayson spoke calmly and rationally, but Lauren didn't like hearing any of it. What kind of life was that for a child? What kind of future would she have? They had no guarantees they could ever completely shut down Romine's crime syndicate. Someone might always be out to harm Lily.

She squeezed her eyes shut. This was one of those things to put in the Lord's hands. It wasn't something she could rectify.

"Lauren, it'll be okay." Grayson had appeared

right beside her. Shayla had disappeared to help interview their captives, and he and Lauren were alone in the living room. He reached a hand out and grasped hers. When she looked into his eyes, she saw strength, empathy and understanding. He was offering her a pillar of support. "I'll make sure of it."

She nodded. "Thank you."

Not just for caring for Lily, but for offering her someone to lean on. She didn't have to say it, though. When he squeezed her hand, she was sure he knew.

Grayson circled their captive one more time, barely containing his fury. "You nearly killed us both, Miss Burris. The least you can do is answer my questions."

She rolled her eyes. "Again, I don't work for Arnie Romine. I can't answer any questions about him."

"Then who do you work for?" Grayson leaned close. "I know you weren't just taking his baby for a joyride."

Cole chimed in. "We've pulled your records, Miss Burris. We know you have a pretty extensive rap sheet. That means you won't be getting a slap on the wrist for your crimes this time. Not unless you want to make a deal."

She slumped. "Okay, look. I have a friend who

used to do a little work for the Romines. He got me on the inside, but I wasn't takin' the kid to Romine." Angelina began to look around nervously, eyes landing on Paretti. "That loser was just supposed to think I was."

"I've done a little research, Miss Burris." Shayla circled the woman, her index finger resting on her lip in thought. "You're with Francisco Harmon… And you used to be Savannah Reid's roommate. You once went by the name Anna Burlington. You were kidnapping the baby to blackmail Romine."

Paretti's face grew red, and he strained against the cuffs that held him to the chair. "You lied?"

Angelina reddened and shrugged.

That only made Paretti angrier. The two began yelling at each other so viciously Grayson couldn't make out half of what they were saying. Curse words and accusations filled the air unhindered, and he had to restrain himself from not covering his ears as their volume increased.

"Mr. Paretti, I thought you said you didn't know who you were working for." Shayla fixed him with a shrewd look.

"I said I didn't have any contact with Romine." He sat back and clamped his mouth shut.

"So you did know it was Romine you were working for." Cole crossed his arms over his chest. "You want your family safe?"

"He's been lying to you the whole time. He's

worked for Romine's gang before." It was Angelina who accused this time, probably trying to take the heat off of herself.

Shayla turned it back on her. "Oh? And how would you know that, Miss Burris?"

Now it was Angelina's turn to become sullen and silent.

"She knows because she used to work for them, too, until she hooked up with Harmon and they split from the gang. He's stupid to trust her, though." Paretti couldn't seem to resist blurting the information, despite the fact that he was incriminating himself further.

Angelina began yelling at him again and another argument ensued between the two.

"Enough!" Grayson roared the word and both captives sat back in wide-eyed attention. He needed to think, but he had no time. This baby was caught in the middle of a three-way war for dominance. How would they ever get this mess lined out? He couldn't even be sure he was getting accurate information out of these two.

First things first—he had to find the baby's mother. She was the key to all of this. Savannah Reid was the one person connected to both gangs as well as Senator Reid. She was the pivotal link to bringing them all into submission.

"Where's Savannah Reid?" He directed the quiet question to Angelina. "You're still in contact with her." He didn't know that for sure, but he thought she might be. A bluff would prove his theory one way or the other.

"I don't know what you're talking about." Angelina looked away.

"Yes, you do. She doesn't know. She still trusts you, doesn't she? She doesn't know you betrayed her." His voice was dead calm. Cole and Shayla just stood back and watched. "She's been gone awhile because of the pregnancy and she doesn't know about what happened with you and Harmon. Am I right?"

Tears welled in her eyes. "I didn't betray her, okay? It wasn't like that. Franco— He—he said we were just starting a new business. We were in too deep before I realized it. He charmed me into going along with his plan with the baby. I didn't think it would hurt Savannah. I thought we could still be friends."

"Was that before or after you tried to kidnap her baby?" Grayson's voice held no compassion. "I think you're lying. You intended to betray Savannah all along."

Angelina's voice rose. "I had no choice!" She leaned forward as she screamed the words. "You don't get it. I had no choice. It was Arnie's fault. And I wanted to get back at him for what he did to Franco."

Grayson circled her chair again. "Look, we

aren't especially interested in your boyfriend's little family gang right now. That's not our turf. But we can help you if you help us. Where do we find Savannah Reid?"

Angelina's gaze shifted. She looked at Shayla standing at the far edge of the room, around to Cole, Paretti and back to Grayson. Her mouth opened and shut. Then she shook her head.

Shayla stepped forward. "Angelina. Woman to woman, we are talking about a child here. I know you have some maternal instincts buried in there somewhere. Don't you think Savannah should have some say over what happens to the baby? *Her* baby? Think about how you would feel if that were your child."

Angelina blinked, her tears flowing again. "She doesn't want to be found. She knew when she found out she was pregnant that something like this would happen. Do you know she wasn't going to keep the baby until Romine found out? He talked her into keeping the baby—said Senator Reid's grandbaby could solve all their problems. They could convince him to give them the money they needed to get out of the country." Her eyes narrowed and she looked back at Grayson. "No child should be used as a pawn."

"I won't argue there. But the baby is going to be in constant danger until we find her mother." Grayson stared her down.

For a long time, she sat completely silent. Grayson turned to Shayla and Cole with a frown. His expression invited further suggestions, but they offered none.

"I can give you an address." Angelina's voice barely penetrated his thoughts, it was so quiet. "But I can't promise you she's still there."

Lily was inconsolable. Lauren knew more from instinct than nursing skill that something was wrong. Her temperature hadn't risen, but the child fussed about everything and nothing. Lauren offered gas relief drops, changed her diaper, offered her a bottle, massaged her tiny tummy, and rocked and sang to her.

Nothing helped.

Grayson had been up to tell her the interrogation had offered a little bit of hope, but had given her few details, and the marshals were all still holed up with their captives. Carlos and Jeff had departed shortly after Grayson and Cole had returned with Angelina. They had accompanied a team to investigate the address Angelina had given them but hadn't reported back yet. Exhaustion pricked at Lauren's form, relentlessly reminding her that she hadn't slept or eaten the way she should in the last forty-eight hours. And this day had seemed never-ending.

Bringing the baby's carrier into the kitchen,

Lauren decided Lily was just going to have to cry long enough for her to scrounge up something for all of them to eat. The marshals were too busy to worry about it right now, so it was up to her. Cole stood guard with Lauren, but he was his usual quiet self and, if possible, even more wary of the baby than Grayson. She placed the fussy infant in the carrier and began to dig through the household groceries. The food consisted of various odds and ends, along with a lot of boxed mixes and frozen options. Lauren finally decided she had what she needed to put together some tacos.

She had started cooking the meat and moved on to chopping the lettuce when a car coming into the drive caught her eye. Cole had slipped down the hall for a minute, leaving her momentarily alone, and she panicked.

She grabbed Lily from the carrier and went to the doorway to call for Cole. When he appeared, she addressed the issue. "Are you expecting company? It's an unmarked car."

"Only one? They were supposed to bring two to pick up both captives." Cole approached to see what she was looking at out the window.

"I only saw one car. I hope they didn't run into any trouble." Lauren followed him through the living room, Lily still fussing and whining.

Grayson appeared at the top of the stairs, just as Lily's fussing escalated into a cry.

When Grayson looked at her questioningly, she shook her head. "I don't really know what's wrong. She doesn't have a temp and I've tried everything to make her comfortable. Nothing works."

She moved away from the window with the infant, closer to Grayson.

"Maybe she's just sleepy? Or has an upset stomach?" Grayson looked uncomfortable standing close to the fussy baby. How could he so easily handle dangerous criminals yet be afraid of an infant? It was almost comical.

"I don't know. She's been like this for a while."

He shook his head in concern, but the marshals in charge of transporting one of the detainees were at the door. Cole showed them in and asked about the other car.

"They should be pulling in any minute. They left a bit behind us," the older, gray-haired marshal explained, not looking so happy to be there.

The gray-haired marshal loaded Paretti into the car, but the other vehicle still hadn't arrived.

"Something's not right." Grayson was on the phone in an instant. He explained to someone on the other end that the second car had never arrived. When he hung up, he went outside. It was only a moment before he returned.

"I asked them to hold up for a few minutes. I have headquarters checking the missing car's location and they'll get back to us. Meanwhile, the safest thing is for the other car to stay put." As Grayson explained, Cole nodded.

Lauren was concerned for the other officers, but her patience with the fussing baby was wearing thin. "I'm going to try to get Lily down for a nap. I've turned out all the fires on the stove and the food is ready. Let me know if there's something I can do."

Lily fought sleep, but finally went down just before Grayson came into the room. His expression was grim in the dim afternoon light. Lauren followed him out of the room and closed the door before he spoke.

"The officers that were supposed to pick up Angelina Burris have disappeared. Cole and Shayla are going out to help search. I need you to stay extra alert for anything unusual."

Lauren's breath caught at his words. "What do you mean they've disappeared?"

"We aren't sure yet. The car, the officers—all seem to have gone missing. The GPS signal went out and there's no trace of them on the road between here and there." Grayson looked angry, even in the semidarkness.

"Will you need to help?" Lauren realized how quiet the house had suddenly become.

"It's a possibility. But I won't leave you here alone. Someone has to protect you and Lily. We can't leave you vulnerable." Grayson looked toward the door where the baby slept, his dark lashes fluttering in concern.

"I know you'll protect us, Grayson." She put a hand on his arm, and when he glanced down at it, she suddenly felt self-conscious and awkward being alone with him.

Before she could pull away, he reached up and clasped her hand. "You've been so brave, Lauren. I know this can't be easy for you." He paused. "I hope it will all be over soon, and you can go back to your normal life."

Normal life… She wasn't really sure what that was anymore. Just the day-to-day, going to work, spending her free time alone? She had thought she wanted to go back to that but…

For some reason, the thought didn't hold as much appeal to her anymore—going home alone to her DC apartment, working long hospital hours and occasionally going out with friends. She was starting to realize what an empty existence she had been living. But she smiled and nodded anyway.

"I really appreciate all you're doing for us, Grayson." She let go of his hand, not wanting to cling, even if he was offering comfort.

Her hand fell back to her side. He gave her a look she couldn't quite interpret. "Just doing my job."

Just doing my job.

Grayson's words echoed back to him as he paced

the back deck. How cheesy had that sounded? And how stupid was he that it wasn't true, that Lauren and Lily were actually getting under his skin? How could he have let this happen?

He knew better than to catch feelings for *any* woman, especially not a witness. This was ridiculous. He had to get over it.

Lord, You know this isn't how I operate on a case. I need Your help here. Please help me get things back on track. He prayed silently while looking up into the bright stars. *And no matter what, protect Lauren and Lily. There are some things I can't do.*

The prayer solidified in his heart. There *were* some things he couldn't do, as much as he hated to admit it. But he knew the One who could.

The woods around them were eerily quiet, except for the sounds of late spring insects and frogs renewing their presence along the lakeshore. There wasn't a lot of activity anywhere nearby, but the night stars sparkled off the water here and there through the trees. An occasional late-evening fisherman cruised past in a bass boat, but the summer fun crowd had yet to make an appearance for the season.

Grayson had been camping with family in his youth, though, and the sights, sounds and smells carried a hint of nostalgia in the night air. Their surroundings brought back so many memories of his mother before her addiction had taken over her life and robbed him of her presence.

He swept the reminiscences away. That wasn't something he wanted to think about right now.

He still hadn't heard anything from Cole and Shayla on the missing officers, and his unease was growing. By now Romine and the Harmon gang knew the marshals had their people in custody.

His thoughts weighed on him, heavily emphasized by the dark night and heavy air. The humidity settled on him, along with the heaviness of impending problems. He often felt this way when a case was about to get more complicated.

The back door opened.

He had sensed Lauren's presence at the door leading to the back porch before she'd made a sound. He wanted to think it was just good instincts from his career in law enforcement, but somehow he knew that, with Lauren, it was something more. He turned and his breath caught at the sight of her. He swallowed it back.

He could tell by the worried expression she wore that something was wrong. "What is it?"

Lauren's pale face illuminated the darkness. He could sense the concern radiating from her in the dark of the moonless night. She was all he could see in the wash of light from the living room lamp.

"It's Lily. She's sick. I think she may have RSV. It's a respiratory condition common in infants that can quickly become serious. Remember, I mentioned it to you earlier? We have to get her to the emergency room, and quickly."

"You're sure? Leaving this house is a big risk right now." The kidnapper's men were undoubtedly lying in wait, ready to pounce on any opportunity to sweep in and nab the baby.

"I know, but I wouldn't ask if it wasn't completely necessary. I don't have any way of keeping her oxygen levels up without a doctor's help. She will need breathing treatments. The longer we wait, the sicker she will be. Newborn babies die of this disease far too often." Lauren held the baby close, but Lily seemed so lethargic she was limp. Even in the low light, he could see the blue around her tiny lips.

He fought the unease that swelled within him. They would be taking a huge risk, no matter what. Leaving their secured safe house would provide the kidnappers opportunities to get to them. But staying at the house might endanger Lily's life, as well, if she was truly as sick as Lauren said.

"You're absolutely sure there's no other way? Could we get a doctor to prescribe a course of home treatment for her? Maybe make a house call and bring the needed equipment?"

"We could try. But we run the risk of wasting time she might not have. If it takes too long to get a call through to a doctor, she could die. How much risk are you willing to take?" Lauren's breathing was growing more rapid.

He considered the odds a moment. It was more likely that he could protect Lily en route to the hospital and back than he could provide her with timely medical care. Their leaving was sudden and they might be able to move before anyone could suspect what they were doing.

"Get everything ready to go. I will make a few necessary arrangements. I have to inform the hospital of the situation ahead of time so they can be prepared. We need to get her there as quickly as possible." He was tapping a number into his phone even as he spoke.

Lauren shuddered. "You think they are just waiting, hoping we will make a move?"

Grayson bit back his frustration. He was doing all he could to keep Lily safe, but everything seemed to be working against him. This might prove to be his biggest challenge yet. He knew there was no way this sort of thing had been caused by anything but natural immune response, but it was almost too convenient for the would-be kidnappers.

He nodded in response to Lauren's question, though. "Getting her to the hospital is going to be the easy part. Coming home will be the riskiest."

The abductors might not expect the move to the hospital, but based on past instances, he was almost certain the people after Lily would know everything they needed to know to plan another attempted kidnapping by the time Lily was discharged from the hospital.

"And you still haven't heard anything from Shayla and Cole?" Lauren looked as anxious as he felt.

"Nothing at all. I tried both cell numbers, but they went to voice mail." Grayson turned to go inside.

"Maybe that's a good sign. They could be busy…" Lauren let her thought trail off. She was probably thinking of all the other negative outcomes he had already considered.

"As soon as you have Lily's things ready, we'll go. I'll grab the keys." He never acknowledged her words.

They reached the nearest hospital without incident. And while the rural emergency staff had given them trouble at first over their lack of proof of guardianship for the baby, when they found out Grayson was a US marshal, everything was worked out in record time.

Once the baby was in triage, Lauren explained that she worked as a NICU nurse and what she believed the symptoms pointed to. The hospital staff contacted the pediatrician on call and began paperwork to check Lily into the PICU. It was a small hospital, but they were proving to be professional and efficient.

Grayson noticed Lauren watched them closely. He was beyond relieved to have her there, knowing how to take care of things for the tiny baby. The whole thing scared him witless.

Lauren must have read his anxiety, for as soon as the other nurses cleared the room, she put a hand on his arm. "She will be okay. She just needs good medical care—care that she couldn't receive without access to the equipment available at a hospital." She gestured at the machines and monitors the staff was already beginning to use for the baby. As soon as they had noted Lily's low pulse ox, the nurses had supplied her with oxygen to bring her levels back up again.

"I'm sure you're right. This is all just new to me." As he looked around at all the hospital equipment, flashes of memory came to him. He had been in a small hospital much like this one when he'd learned that his mother had nearly died in a car accident. Her injuries had been extensive, leaving her with lasting damage. She had taken painkillers for a long time after multiple surgeries and ended up addicted. That addiction had sent her into a downward spiral that had eventually taken her from him altogether.

Emotion pressed in on him now—all the shortcomings he had felt as a fourteen-year-old boy, knowing he couldn't do anything to help his mother, and again later, that he couldn't make her love him enough to give up the pills. He and his brothers had argued more than once about which one of them had driven her to her addiction. He hadn't lost hope that she would one day come back until he was much older. As he matured into adulthood, however, he finally realized the bitter truth. And even when he'd understood that there had been nothing any of them could have done to save her from her dependence, it hurt terribly knowing she had been released from prison and never come back to them.

Looking at Lily's tiny form, struggling to breathe, he felt that same helplessness. He couldn't help her. He wasn't enough. He was just fooling himself if he thought he would ever be enough for her or for Lauren. All he could do was protect them with his life. That was all he *should* be trying to do. Where had he gotten this image of them as a family that kept trying to resurface in his mind?

He had to get this case back on track, and he had to do it now.

Lauren watched Grayson leave the small hospital room and had to force back her questions. It was apparent from his expression that he needed a moment, and as much as she wanted to know what was wrong, pushing him for answers wouldn't help. Besides, she needed to focus on making sure the baby received the best treatment possible until she was well.

A few other members of the hospital staff ventured in and out, but Grayson never returned. Curious, she finally stuck her head out the door.

He hadn't left them after all. He was leaning up against the wall right outside, watching every person who came and went. It wasn't lost on Lauren that he was occupying his nervous energy by being extra protective. She just had no idea what was making him so apprehensive.

"Is everything okay? Lily—" He sprang to attention when he saw her.

"Everything's fine." Lauren smiled to back up her words. "I just didn't know where you were. They are taking her to a private room soon and I wanted to be sure you knew."

"Thanks. I finally heard back from Shayla and Cole. They still haven't found the other car, but the search for it has been called off for the time being. The marshals were found safe, bound in the woods, but the men who took their car drugged them. They don't remember much aside from the all-black clothing they wore. Shayla and Cole are back at the safe house."

"Why do you think they took their car? What would be the point of that?" Lauren looked confused at the idea.

"I can't be sure, but I assume they have some plan that involves impersonating law enforcement. They took their badges and US Marshal Kevlar vests from the trunk."

"Oh. That isn't good." Lauren's face blanched.

Grayson nodded. "All the more reason we need to be on constant watch."

At that moment, a tall, red-haired physician strode down the hall toward them. Pausing at Lily's door, she stretched out a hand to Lauren. "Hello. I'm Dr. Claremont. Are you the mother of the infant?"

"No, we are her temporary guardians, actually." Lauren gestured between herself and Grayson. "It's complicated."

Dr. Claremont looked from Lauren to Grayson in surprise. "How so?"

Grayson stepped forward and showed his badge. "The baby is in the protective custody of the US Marshals Service. It's a sensitive situation. We wouldn't be here if she wasn't very sick. I called and spoke to someone before we arrived."

"Of course." Dr. Claremont leaned in, assessing him as well as the badge. "It was my colleague Dr. Shaw you spoke to. Everything is ready for you. We'd better get to it."

The doctor took them into an exam room. She began looking over the baby and, when she had finished, sat at a computer to enter information into Lily's charts. "It's a good thing you got here when you did. Respiratory illnesses like this one can be deadly in a newborn."

"Lauren is a NICU nurse in DC." Grayson's voice held an odd note of pride and Lauren's cheeks warmed. "She knew what to watch for. She probably saved her life."

Dr. Claremont looked up at Grayson, then over at Lauren. A knowing smile curved her lips. "Well, this little one is grateful, I'm sure. Let's get her into a private room. I see the nurses have started breathing treatments at the behest of the ER doctor?"

"Yes, her pulse ox levels have already risen significantly." Lauren gave the doctor some information on Lily's vitals previous to their arrival and they collaborated a moment on the baby's overall health and treatment options. Grayson looked a little lost.

A young nurse burst in, breathless and looking a little harried. "Dr. Claremont, there's a…a man at the front desk demanding to be shown to the newborn's room. He says he knows she's here. He's wearing a jacket that says US Marshal, and he flashed a badge, but there's something odd about the way he's acting. He's getting impatient. What do I do? The receptionist needs help. We've called security."

Lauren's heart began to race. Romine's men had found them.

Grayson answered before the doctor could respond. "Call the police. Try to keep him calm until the police can get here." The nurse nodded and scurried out. Grayson looked at Lauren. "You help get Lily to a private room ASAP. Make sure it is as secure as possible."

Dr. Claremont paged in as many members of the ER and PICU staff as she could reasonably gather. "Get this baby to room 406 in the PICU stat. Secure the area. No one goes in or out without my express permission. Tell any staff members that aren't here. Go, people. Now."

Before Lauren could get Lily moving in the direction of the private room, yelling in the corridor spurred everyone into action. A child in the waiting area started to cry and a woman tried to calm him. Lauren had moved to the door of the exam room, looked in that direction and froze.

One of the nurses took Lily from Lauren and headed toward an elevator.

Grayson turned to look in the direction of the yelling. The man was heading their way. He wasn't anyone Grayson knew, and he suspected he wasn't even a marshal. He wore a determined expression as he closed in on him. Grayson had his hand on his gun. His hesitation was visible. He turned to

Lauren and motioned toward the nurses following Lily out of sight.

"Go with her, Ms. Beck. I'll send your marshal to you as soon as he gets the situation under control." Dr. Claremont urged her toward the baby being taken onto a private elevator. Lauren's feet still didn't want to cooperate. Her marshal? What had given the doctor that idea? The ruckus in the corridor continued. Lauren stretched and strained her head to see what was happening around the corner where the reception desk was located. She couldn't see Grayson anymore, so she made her way out into the hall a little farther. A woman down the corridor screamed.

"He has a gun!"

"Everyone down!" Grayson's voice issued the command.

A gunshot fired about the time Lauren felt a vicious bite in her upper arm. Pain seared through her flesh, sharp and unrelenting. Darkness clawed at her and she stumbled, clutching at her arm.

The faint sounds of a struggle came to her as if from far away and she caught the wall to her right to help brace herself. People began to surround her, talking and asking questions, none of which quite penetrated her fog.

Confusion swam around her. She pulled her right hand from the flaming left arm and looked down. She knew the sight of blood. It was familiar.

But it was everywhere. And this time it was her own. Reality finally began to penetrate. It wasn't a dream. It hurt too much.

She had been shot.

EIGHT

Grayson saw Lauren stumble into the wall, clutching her arm as a red stain spread over her sleeve. His throat constricted. Rage filled him and he had the gunman secure in one fluid movement. By the time the police arrived, he had the man cuffed and on his feet. He did little more than shove him in the direction of the officers before sprinting for the area the medical staff had taken Lauren.

Reassuring himself first that the nurses had Lily's care well in hand, he stuck his head in every door until he found Lauren, sitting up on a hospital bed behind a blue curtain. An ER doctor was prodding at her arm, yet she offered him a smile when she saw him, then winced slightly.

"Lauren." He looked her up and down, making sure she was truly okay.

"I'm fine, Grayson. It just grazed my arm. Dr. Stover numbed it to ease the pain and he's going to get me bandaged up." She still looked pale and frightened, despite her words. He wasn't sure she was really fine.

"Actually, it might need a couple of stitches, just to close up this deep spot in the middle." Dr. Stover was a young guy with blond hair and glasses.

Grayson looked her over one more time. "You're sure you're okay?"

"She'll be fine." The doctor smiled at Lauren, and Grayson felt a twinge of jealousy, despite his earlier conversation with himself. He also kind of wanted to tell Dr. Stover that he was talking to Lauren, not him, but he snapped his mouth shut on that remark.

Instead, he did what he had to do. He was on the job. "Then I'm going to go check on Lily. She's been without the two of us for too long."

Lauren nodded. "I'm sorry. This is my fault. I should have been with her. I couldn't get my feet moving. I don't know what happened. I just froze."

"I'm sure she's fine." He turned and almost fled the room.

He was suffocating. She *should* have stayed out of the corridor, but he was too angry to confront her in front of Dr. Goo-Goo Eyes in there.

And what was wrong with him that he didn't want the young doctor admiring Lauren's beauty? It didn't matter to him. Did it?

He strode to the elevators but then took the

stairs instead. He needed to do something physical to help work this off.

When he arrived at the PICU, the new nurse he encountered made him show her his badge and ID, which made him feel a little better about Lily's safety. He entered the private room to find the infant connected to a host of machines and monitors. She looked even tinier in the high-slatted crib with the various wires and tubes surrounding her. She was asleep, but he needed to make sure she was really fine.

"Can I touch her?" The question was for the petite nurse standing behind him.

"Sure. We encourage parents to keep physical contact. It comforts the babies and speeds healing." The nurse seemed to remember hearing something about the baby's situation then. She paused, as if not quite sure how to proceed. "I mean, even if you aren't her father, you're probably the closest she has right now."

Grayson considered that. Lily really didn't have anything closer to a parent right now than him and Lauren. It made his heart ache for the beautiful little baby. Her full pink lips puckered in sleep as he laid a gentle hand on her tummy. Sure, she frightened him a little, but it was only because she was so tiny and seemingly fragile. He thought of how easily Lauren handled her and felt a pang. She should be here with Lily. That man should have never been able to get off a shot. The idea that Lauren had been injured because he hadn't secured the gunman sooner made his chest seize; he couldn't even consider how he would feel if something worse had happened to her.

The door creaked open and he turned to see a nurse wheeling Lauren into the room.

Lauren gave him a slightly loopy grin. "They wouldn't let me walk." She shrugged in an exaggerated motion. "I don't know why. I got shot in the arm, not the leg."

The nurse with her rolled his eyes. "Maybe because you were running into walls after we gave you that pain medication."

Lauren giggled. "Just one."

The nurse gave Grayson a look that said Lauren had run into more than one wall. Instead of arguing, however, he helped Lauren into a chair near Lily's crib. She stumbled a little and practically fell into the seat.

"Oops!" She giggled again as she flopped into the chair.

"She's all yours. Have fun." The nurse shook his head before wheeling out the empty chair.

"Wow, Lauren. What'd they give you?" Grayson couldn't quite suppress his smile.

She stopped examining something interesting on the ceiling tiles and looked at him. She grinned. "The good stuff."

He couldn't keep from laughing then. "I guess you would know."

She poked clumsily at her arm. "I didn't feel a thing."

He pulled her hand away gently. "Easy. You might feel it later."

She blinked, then looked at the crib. "How's Lily?"

"About the same. She's sleeping."

"Hmm." Lauren dragged the sound out and nodded slowly.

"I think you should also probably rest."

But his words were wasted. Her eyes had already drifted closed and her head slumped against the back of the chair.

"A shame." He chuckled to himself. "This could have been pretty entertaining."

Lauren woke a little disoriented, with a crick in her neck, but that was mild compared to the flaming pain in her upper arm. She started to rise and gasped.

Grayson raised his head and looked her way, a little sleepy-eyed, as well. "Lauren, do you need something?"

"It just hurts pretty badly." She tried to keep her face serene, but she couldn't hold back the wince. She pressed her lips together.

"I'll have them bring you something else for the

pain." Grayson stood from his place in the other chair by Lily's crib.

"No, no. I'll be okay." Lauren shook her head.

"I've been shot before. Trust me when I say you're going to need meds. You don't wanna try to tough this one out." He went to the door before she could protest any further, but she caught the expression of pain that flashed across his handsome features.

What was that about?

Lauren realized, watching him go, that there were a great many things she didn't know about Grayson. He revealed little about himself to her, and she found she was curious. Why had he chosen this dangerous profession? Where had he grown up? What did he do when he wasn't working? Why wasn't he married?

Whoa. Where had that last thought come from? That was way too personal for her to wonder about a casual acquaintance. And despite the close quarters they had found themselves in for the last few days, that was still really all they were—right?

When he returned, Lauren dismissed the thoughts. If she were truthful, her thoughts had scattered on their own at the sight of him. Though he wasn't smiling, she had come to recognize the stern expression he wore as relaxed for him.

"They should be here with your meds in just a few minutes."

Before she could respond, there was a little squeak from Lily's crib, and the baby began to fuss. Lauren started to get up, then winced again. Grayson strode to the crib and began to soothe the baby, talking to her in a quiet voice. Lauren watched in awe as he stroked her little belly and the baby calmed.

Lauren hadn't heard the nurse enter, but she spoke quietly from behind her. "He got her to sleep doing that before you got here."

Lauren turned to look at her. "Really?"

The petite nurse nodded and handed her a small plastic cup with a huge white pill in it. "He's good with her." She moved past Lauren to the crib. "Let me check her vitals while she's awake."

After a few moments of working on and around the baby, taking her temperature and reading monitors, the nurse, named Hannah, nodded at them. "Her fever's down. She's already showing signs of improvement. Keep up the good work."

When she was gone, Lauren took the pain medicine with the water the nurse had handed her. Grayson watched her a moment before speaking his thoughts. "I know Lily is pretty safe here right now, but we have to get her out of here soon."

"I'm sure the kidnapper's men will be waiting for us to leave. The longer we stay, the more we put innocent people in danger. But do we take her back to the cabin?" Lauren's face twisted into a frown.

"I haven't decided. But we do have to get her out of here before they get any more desperate. Do you think she is healthy enough to manage outside of the hospital now that we have her meds?" Grayson looked doubtful.

"I think she's a strong fighter, and I know how to take care of her. We'll get the doctor to prescribe her a strong course of treatment for home, and if we must, we'll find another hospital." Lauren looked around. It had been a good place to get treatment for Lily and she hated to go, but she knew it was in everyone's best interest.

Grayson intended to watch Lauren's use of the pain meds carefully. He knew not everyone had his mother's issues, but the less time Lauren had to depend on them, the better. Hopefully, the short-term, low dosage would keep her comfortable, but not give her enough time to form an attachment.

She didn't seem to notice his preoccupation with it. He had told the truth. He had needed the meds after being shot, but he had weaned himself off as soon as he could.

It was several hours later before Grayson had convinced Dr. Claremont to release Lily into Lauren's care. Cole and Shayla met them at the doors to the PICU. Hannah, their amazing nurse, helped them with all the equipment they would need to take care of Lily's breathing treatments at home.

The hospital had prescribed a nebulizer that would assist with helping Lily breathe and given Lauren careful instructions on how to reach the doctor if Lily worsened in any way. Grayson carried the baby.

"So far we're clear. Nothing suspicious." Cole led the way out. It was just after two o'clock, and Lauren's pain meds must have worn off. She was much more lucid and followed Grayson with the rest of Lily's things.

Even though the staff moved around, it was eerily quiet in the hospital, the fluorescent lights shining too brightly and buzzing too loudly in the silence. Their footsteps, harsh and unwelcoming, echoed along the empty corridor, and hospital staff looked at them curiously as they passed.

"Get Lily and Lauren settled while we keep watch." Cole spoke the soft words just as they reached the SUV. Cole had switched his own vehicle for the one with Lily's car seat. Rather than take two cars, Cole would drive while Shayla and Grayson kept a lookout for trouble.

Grayson helped Lauren settle Lily in the car seat, then allowed Lauren to fasten all the straps from inside the vehicle. They were about to jump in when two black vans with darkly tinted windows pulled in. One stopped in front and the other behind them.

Grayson had to prod Lauren into movement as

she froze beside the vehicle. He ushered her into the SUV.

"Lock the doors." Grayson directed the order toward Lauren and pulled his Glock, aiming it at the van in front of the SUV. Cole was calling the police on his cell. Shayla had her gun aimed at the dark van behind them.

Lauren watched from behind the tinted glass, shielding Lily. He saw her lips moving and thought she might be praying.

Two men jumped from each of the vehicles, wielding weapons of their own.

"We don't want to shoot you. We just want the baby," one of the men said aggressively as he approached. "Hand over the kid and no one will get hurt."

Grayson shook his head. "You're not getting your hands on that child." He lowered his aim and fired a shot next to the man's left foot. The man jumped back with a yelp but didn't get back in the van.

"These guys must be getting paid a lot of money," Shayla muttered beside him.

She was right. They weren't going to give up easily.

"We can't let you leave until you give us the kid. If you don't cooperate, we will have to kill you." One of the other guys was talking this time. He said it smoothly, as if it were an everyday thing.

"Not gonna happen. How exactly do you think you'll pull that off?" Grayson was trying to keep them talking until backup arrived.

"There are three of you and four of us." He gestured at the three marshals, all now holding guns on them. "Odds are at least one of us survives, but all of you are dead."

"What if you accidentally shoot the baby? How're you gonna get your money then?" It was Shayla with this argument.

No one spoke for a moment.

"I doubt all of you actually shoot that well." Cole chuckled. "That makes the odds a little different."

A reckless fury came over the guy's face, and as he stepped toward them, Shayla shot at his foot, hitting the target smoothly. He began to howl in pain, falling to the ground, his weapon clattering to the asphalt.

"Oh, look. The odds have been evened up." Shayla grinned.

"Quit messing around! Just get the kid and let's get going—" This third man's voice sounded a little panicked as sirens wailed in the distance, almost before he could get the demand out.

He let out a curse. "Let's go!"

The guy Shayla had shot in the foot began to whine. "Hey, somebody help me. I can't get in the van like this! Come on!"

One of the bigger men grabbed him with one arm, still pointing his gun at the marshals with the hand of the other. He dragged the wounded man to the van as he screamed the whole way. "Shut up or I'll just leave you here for the cops."

The rest of the men backed toward their respective vans, as well. They held their guns aimed on the marshals until they had closed the doors on the vans and peeled off, police cars giving chase.

When they were out of sight, Grayson motioned for Lauren to unlock the doors. "That was close."

Lauren was trembling. "Too close," she replied. Lily was beginning to fuss. The marshals loaded into the SUV, Grayson taking the vacant seat on the other side of Lily's carrier. Lauren felt his eyes scan her before looking over Lily to see how the baby fared.

"Don't waste any time. We need to get Lily out of here." Grayson was instructing Cole, who had taken the wheel. Lauren didn't register all of his instructions. She was too focused on Lily.

"No problem." Cole glanced back to be sure everyone was ready and put the SUV in gear.

They made it a few miles before another van started following them, this one white.

"That didn't take long." Shayla, riding shotgun, pulled her weapon. "Can I shoot out his tires?"

"No shooting." Grayson growled the order. "We just need to lose them."

The town was fairly small and there wasn't much of anywhere to go. When a second white van joined the chase, it became obvious they wouldn't be able to return to the lake house anymore. Grayson grumbled out the news, making Lauren wonder why he might want to stay. But the kidnappers were desperate. It was time to move.

"I'm calling for the plane. We have to get this baby out of here," Grayson declared. Neither Cole nor Shayla argued. Lauren felt ill.

Grayson had been put on hold and turned to explain to Lauren that the Marshals Service had private planes for just such a purpose, but they just had to get to the aircraft safely.

Once he disconnected, Grayson leaned forward to talk to Cole, keeping his gun drawn and ready. "The nearest private airstrip is about an hour away. Do you think we can ever get there?"

Cole jerked his chin in an affirmative motion. Lauren thought he looked kind of happy about the challenge. "Oh, yeah. Just let me lose these goobers."

The two white vans sped closer, trying to force them into stopping by swerving in front of them and hitting the brakes. Lauren's unsettled stomach protested anew.

"Right. Well, could you do it soon? I'm getting

a little tired of hitting my head on the roof every time you swerve." Shayla grabbed for the handle above her with her right hand. Cole was doing the best he could, but Lauren was in complete agreement with Shayla. She wasn't enjoying this ride.

Cole practically growled at her. "Don't you think I'm working on it?"

Shayla wasn't at all intimidated. "Well, work faster. You're probably making the baby dizzy."

"Why don't you drive and I'll navigate?" He let go of the wheel as if to prove a point.

"Cole!" Shayla grabbed the wheel.

"*Somebody* better drive. While you two are flirting, the bad guys are gaining on us." Grayson gave them both a look that said they'd better straighten up.

Cole took back the wheel.

Lauren knew the marshals were in control, but her pulse was racing and she felt ill. The sweet scent of the lotion the nurses had used on Lily at the hospital after giving her a cooling bath heightened her nausea. She closed her eyes, praying that this would be over soon and she would have Lily safely in her arms.

Grayson's solid presence was a comfort, though, and the way he kept giving her concerned glances, as if to assure himself she was okay, made her insides go a little soft. He looked so fiercely handsome directing Cole and watching the kidnappers to anticipate their next move.

She watched as Grayson punched a number into his phone and, after a brief conversation, reported to Cole and Shayla. "We have state troopers en route to help us."

It couldn't have been as long as it seemed, but finally the sirens became audible. Relief swept through Lauren and she thought Grayson's relief was almost tangible also.

The vans chasing them skidded to a stop and Cole floored it on out of town.

When they were finally in the clear, Cole spoke to Grayson over his shoulder. "Get me a route on GPS."

Grayson already had it pulled up. He started giving Cole directions. "Don't waste any time. They'll regroup and be right back on our tail in no time."

"Not if I can help it." Cole drove with almost obsessive concentration, but it was a pretty good while before Lauren could fully release the breath she was holding.

She just didn't know how much more of this constant adrenaline she could handle.

To Grayson's amazement, they drove for almost a full hour without incident. He knew, however, that things were about to go in a different direction. In a situation like this, when villains were quiet, a more elaborate plan was likely being hatched.

They were close to the private airstrip where the plane sat fueled up and ready, and Grayson was growing anxious again, his senses heightened. Lauren's shampoo wafted toward him as she turned to adjust Lily's blanket, and he couldn't help but be aware of her, despite his desire to keep his distance. She was everything good in this life and he felt a tenderness for her welling up in him, much like the tenderness she was showing toward Lily as she gently smoothed the blanket. He wanted to shield them from all this, but right now, he just had to keep them safe.

He forced his thoughts to return to the task at hand.

"You're about five minutes out, but we're going to go around the back way and enter through a service entrance. I don't like how quiet our bad guys have been." Grayson leaned up and checked on Cole, then handed Shayla his phone.

"Roger that. I won't relax until we're in the air," he agreed. Grayson half expected Shayla to quip about Cole's inability to relax ever, but she remained silent, studying the phone in her hand.

Lily still slept, most likely lulled into a deep, restful state by the medicine and the illness. He knew that Lauren watched the baby very closely, rarely taking her eyes from the infant for more than a second. She had to be exhausted and her arm must hurt terribly, though she never uttered a complaint.

They pulled up to the back gate and showed a man their badges. Grayson had called to let airport security know they would be entering that way, so the man at the gate had been expecting them.

"Be prepared. The kidnapper and his men have been staying one step ahead of us." Grayson little more than had the words out when the prickles started.

"Grayson?" Cole must have felt it, too.

"Stay right here. I'm calling for backup."

At that, an army of automatic-rifle-armed people started coming out of the woods around the airstrip, moving closer to the SUV as a single entity.

"Whaaaa—? How did they get in?" Shayla sounded as freaked out as the rest of them had to be feeling.

As the line of armed men closed in, another line of rifle-bearing men emerged from the other side of the airstrip.

"Someone knew where we were headed." Cole gritted the words out through his teeth.

"How do they keep finding us?" Lauren's voice was pitched high with fear.

"There is only one way they could be staying one step ahead of us." Grayson's eyes met

Shayla's and she nodded. She handed his phone back wordlessly.

"Only the Marshals Service has access to our GPS. It's blocked to everyone else." Cole voiced aloud what Grayson meant.

"So you really do think there is a leak?" Lauren spoke so softly, she seemed afraid of the words themselves.

The SUV was deathly silent for a moment before Grayson answered. "It would seem so."

"But who?" Lauren asked.

"It's hard to tell. My guess is the marshal assigned to Savannah Reid might have a good idea." Grayson was looking over the assembly of armed men on the parking lot. "But we don't have a name."

The rest of the questions would have to wait. The attention of everyone in the SUV was drawn to the situation at hand.

The two sides eyed each other, even as they watched the SUV. What was that about? Something strange was going on here.

Grayson was on the phone trying to get some backup, but Shayla and Cole continued to converse while Lauren just listened in.

"Cole, something weird is going on. Look, some of them are turning their guns on each other." Shayla leaned forward as she looked out the window.

Grayson lost track of some of the conversation

going on in the SUV while he reported what was going on, but when he disconnected, Lauren was talking.

She gestured to a tall, dark-haired man in a navy blue hoodie. "I recognize him. The news report. He's one of the men from the Harmon gang, wanted for his involvement in the shootings."

"But the guy over here in the gray T-shirt—he's one of Romine's men. He's been in custody before, but they didn't have enough to hold him." This was from Shayla.

"It seems," Grayson began, looking at them both, then back at the armed men, "that we're caught between the two gangs trying to kidnap Romine's baby. There is definitely a leak."

NINE

A chill traveled down Lauren's spine. Memories of the news report she had watched on the previous battle between the rival gangs flashed back to her. They were all in serious danger.

More than half a dozen men on each side squared off on one another. They formed two rows, with the SUV at one end of the rows of men, but not quite between them. It was almost like a movie scene playing in slow motion. The whole thing seemed to unfold before their eyes as the heavy dread filled her chest cavity.

The yelling started just before the gunfire began. The horrible rat-a-tat of the AK-47s pierced her eardrums as Cole threw the SUV into Reverse just in time, peeling out backward through the gate.

The last thing Lauren saw before squeezing her eyes shut was the dropping bodies on both sides of the lines as the AK-47s fired. She felt the vehicle wheel around to go away from the scene.

Shayla was calling 9-1-1 to get paramedics on the way, and Grayson was feeding her details on their location and the number of potential injuries. Lauren thought they were being pursued based on the conversation going on around her, but she couldn't focus on it, nor did she have any idea which side was pursuing them, or if it were both. Not that it mattered.

She swallowed back the thick bile rising in her throat, praying her stomach would calm.

Lily had awakened and began to fuss weakly. The receding sounds of gunfire and shouting seemed surreal to Lauren, and she squeezed her fists closed as she concentrated on her breathing. She spoke in a low and soothing voice to Lily, barely aware of what she was doing. Between the pings of bullets, excited voices and g-force on the passengers of the vehicle, brought on by their rapid acceleration, pressing them hard against the seats, Lily responded unhappily, filling the vehicle with her cries. Lauren spoke softly to the baby, doing her best to calm her.

"Stop." Grayson made the command to Cole in a calm, quiet voice, leading Lauren to wonder if she had imagined it.

"Are you crazy?" Cole never let off the gas.

"Stop. The shooting has stopped. There's no one pursuing us. We need to go back." Grayson sounded completely numb, almost robotic. Was this how he dealt with such incidents?

"Are you sure it's safe? We have a baby in the vehicle." Shayla's voice was also low.

"I'm aware. If it's safe, we still need to board the plane." Grayson held up a hand and Cole finally stopped.

Lauren realized he was right. No one followed them. Everything was quiet. It was eerie. "How do you know it isn't another trap?"

The wailing sirens answered her question. None of the gang members would stick around with police and emergency personnel swarming the place.

"That's going to scatter them if they aren't gone already." Shayla's words echoed her thoughts.

As the SUV pulled back into the airstrip's parking area, she averted her eyes. She didn't want to look at the lifeless bodies or the bullet holes. Scenarios she had only seen on television. The reality of what had happened constricted her lungs.

"Lauren, you and Lily go straight to the plane. I'll do my best to divert any questions from the local police and reporters and get us off the ground quickly. I'm so sorry you had to see this." Grayson squeezed her hand before getting out of the vehicle.

She looked up briefly to nod at him, and then she remembered herself. Though it was a devastating circumstance, she was a trained nurse.

She grabbed for his hand again. "Grayson, I know there probably aren't any survivors, but I'm a trained nurse. Shayla can take care of Lily for a bit if necessary. If there is anyone who needs me…" She let her words trail off. Emergency vehicles had begun to swarm the scene and she realized the EMTs would probably have it covered.

He nodded, though. "Thank you, Lauren."

All the lights around her became a dizzying mass of confusion. The needless loss of life hit her like a blow to the abdomen, and she began to pray for the families and all those affected by this unnecessary massacre. Lily sucked in a little breath and Lauren looked down at her. What would have happened if one gang had gotten to Lily before the other?

Chill bumps prickled along her skin at the idea of the tiny baby caught in the cross fire. The thought just renewed Lauren's determination to protect the child.

Lily was calm and beginning to lull back into a sleep, but Lauren knew she would need a breathing treatment soon, so she unbuckled her and eased her from the carrier while the vehicle was at a standstill. She cradled the baby's tiny, warm form to her chest.

Lauren would be lying to herself if she said she had never thought about having children of her own, but her reluctance to get into a relationship made motherhood and family a foreign dream for her. True, more people in unique family situations were adopting in modern times. But Lauren didn't want to raise a child alone. The challenges of parenting were great, and, in her opinion, a child needed a father.

Thinking about becoming a mother made her wonder about Lily. She couldn't deny she had formed an attachment to the infant. If anything happened to Savannah, who would raise her? Lauren hated to think of anyone else being a mother to Lily, but with no husband and a busy career, how could she even consider raising a child? But she had definitely thought about it, late at night when no one was stirring and at the oddest times, like now, when she should be worrying about other things. What would it be like to be Lily's mother?

Grayson returned to find her singing to Lily after giving her a breathing treatment. "How's she doing?"

"Better than a lot of us." Lauren waved a hand around, indicating the gang members. "Did any of them survive?"

The grimace on his face told her what she needed to know. "There are a few still alive at the moment, but they are all pretty critical."

Lauren couldn't stop the tears from welling up. "I can't stand to see what happened. It's such a needless loss of life. Someone should have reached them, helped them, before it was too late to save their lives. How many of them have ever even heard about God's love?"

"It isn't on you, Lauren. Everyone hates to see these things happen. It's painful to witness the evil wrought on the world by an enemy. The Bible tells us the enemy comes to steal, kill and destroy." Grayson wiped at her tears with amazing gentleness. "We aren't meant to understand some of the tragedies of this life."

She could feel Grayson's eyes on her face.

"You're right, of course. But I can't help thinking of Lily. What if the timing had been different and she had been in the middle of this? It just makes my blood go cold." Lauren shook her head at him, eyes filling with tears.

"God takes care of the innocent ones. We can be thankful for that." He paused a moment. "They are going to clear us for takeoff in about ten to fifteen minutes. I'm sorry we couldn't get more of Lily's and your things. Can you get her by until we land? It will be about an hour flight, maybe a little longer."

"Yes, I think we can manage. Where are we going?" Lauren felt both displaced and weary, but she couldn't stop the questions.

"I'll tell you later. I'm going to go finish finalizing plans and give my statement to the authorities before we get moving again." He hopped out before she could even protest.

"Well, Miss Lily, it seems you're going to see the whole country before you're even old enough to remember it, from the looks of things." Lauren sighed as the baby yawned. She didn't appear to be impressed.

It seemed too soon that Grayson was joining Lauren and Lily in the passenger chamber of the jet as they prepared for takeoff. Lauren had never flown on such a small plane before; in fact, she had only flown once before, and she barely recalled it.

Her nervousness must have been evident.

"It's nothing to worry about. We have the best pilots in the nation." Grayson grinned at her. He took Lily and secured her carrier into the seat beside the one he indicated for Lauren to settle into. Shayla had just boarded the plane and was busy entering something into her phone, and Lauren noted that she missed the marshal's sunny commentary. Shayla stepped back out of the plane then, making Lauren wonder if she was about to be alone with Lily and Grayson again.

"Shayla and Cole are coming, too, right?" Her voice sounded stronger than she felt.

"Yeah, they'll board any minute. Why? Are you still afraid to be alone with me?" Grayson smiled again. She knew he was trying to make this whole situation easier for her, and she appreciated it, but she was still floundering.

She tried to smile back, but the attempt felt weak. "Of course. Now that I've seen firsthand how scary you are, I need backup."

He watched her face. "Seriously, Lauren. I know this is a lot to take in. Are you making it okay?"

She shrugged, but her eyes filled. "I'm okay. As good as can be expected."

"You need a distraction." He sat beside her.

"Okay. You know all my secrets. Tell me about your family." Her voice was slightly teasing, soft.

Grayson hesitated. "You know I have four brothers. Briggs and Beau are twins. Then there is Caldwell, and the baby is Avery. I am the second youngest."

She nodded. "And your parents?"

Darkness clouded his expression. "My dad passed away a few years ago from cancer."

"I'm sorry to hear that." She paused for only a second. "What about your mother?"

He blew out a sigh and his right hand moved over his chest. "She hasn't been in my life since my early teen years."

Lauren just watched him expectantly, hoping he would explain.

"She was in a car accident with a friend. She nearly died. But the recovery process was extremely painful. She took high-powered pain pills for a long time to get through it."

Lauren filled in the blanks. "She became addicted to them."

His expression showed his surprise at her astute assumption.

"I'm a nurse. I know it isn't all that unusual. That's why you watched me so closely with mine."

Grayson just nodded. "Yeah. But she grew desperate for them. She got caught stealing the pills. She ended up in prison for several years. When she got out, she never came home."

"Oh, Grayson, I'm so sorry. She must have had her reasons." She tried to blink back the tears.

Lauren spoke again, not wanting Grayson to feel he had to say any more. "I know it must be hard, but forgiving her would make such a difference in your life. It isn't your fault. And I'm sure she probably misses you and your brothers terribly. No doubt she is ashamed."

"I don't know if I can forgive her. She abandoned us."

"Of course you can, Grayson. You're the strongest, kindest person I've ever known." She grasped his hand.

His arms were around her before she could guess what he was doing.

"I'm sorry this is happening with Lily." He breathed the words against her hair.

Lauren melted into him. His strong arms felt so right around her, and as she breathed in his woodsy, masculine scent, she felt all her tension begin to ease away. She felt safe in his arms, cared for, even.

Her cheek was nestled against his shoulder and she could hear his heart beating. No other embrace had ever felt so perfect and she just wanted to stay there forever.

But she couldn't.

Even if he felt the same way…well, men's feelings were fickle and he would end up wanting to change her and control her, just as her late husband had. She wasn't whole, but she couldn't fix it. She had tried. She just couldn't ever be enough.

She pulled away. "I'm sorry, Grayson. I promised I wouldn't be any trouble, and here I am, needing to be babied."

"Lauren, don't do that. Anyone would be upset by what they'd just seen. It doesn't make you weak. It makes you human." Grayson let her go but didn't move away.

"Then why are you and your fellow marshals just letting it roll off? Not that you don't care, but you just don't seem fazed by it all." Lauren shook her head.

"Because we still have a job to do. We are trained to shut it off until we take care of business. We've all seen too much. I hate to say we are hardened to it, but in a way, I guess we are. At the end of the day, though, don't ever think it doesn't get to us."

"I guess you have to learn to be thick-skinned to work as a marshal or you wouldn't be able to do your job." Lauren gave him a grateful smile. "It isn't that I haven't seen the results of violence. I've had to treat kids for stabbing and gunshot wounds in nursing school rounds. But I've never actually seen anyone get shot firsthand. It was awful."

Grayson helped her settle into her seat. "Well, I haven't seen violence like that often, but I have seen more than enough. Let's talk about something else. Maybe getting your mind off of it for a little while will help. Tell me about your family."

She took a deep breath. "Well, my mother is a paralegal in DC. My father died when I was just six years old. Eventually, my mother remarried—to a lawyer—and they had my younger sister, Britlan, when I was fourteen. My stepfather left not long after Britlan was born, though. They found out she was sick, and my stepfather couldn't handle the pressure of caring for a child that needed so much attention. So my mother and I did it all."

He looked at her in amazement. "Wow. That's a lot to put on a fourteen-year-old." He could relate, but it had been different with his brothers around. They hadn't had a sick sibling to care for.

"It was, but I don't regret it. I got a work permit

and began helping financially as well as physically. I grew to love Britlan like my own child. There are days she can live an almost perfectly normal life. But there are also days she is so sick she can't leave her bed."

"I'm sorry to hear that. How's your mother making it without you right now?" Grayson asked.

"Once I took the job at the hospital, we hired someone to help Britlan part-time, so she isn't having to do it alone. I wish I knew how she's doing, though. I hope no emergencies have come up, because they have no way to contact me."

Grayson winced. "Why don't you give her a call? I should have offered to let you call sooner. I'm really sorry."

"No." Lauren stretched out a hand and placed it on his arm. "It isn't your fault. You had a lot of other things on your mind."

"You should have asked me." Grayson grasped her hand.

She smiled. "We've been a little busy with other things."

"Of course. But you need to keep in touch with your family." Grayson squeezed her fingers. He held out his phone in offering.

"You were trying to do your job. You had just unexpectedly gained custody of a newborn. That's often traumatizing to expectant parents who had nine months to prepare."

His laughter filled the cabin of the plane as she accepted the phone.

"What's so funny?" Shayla ducked into the cabin.

"We were just discussing parenting." Lauren grinned.

"More like how I know nothing about it." Grayson made a face.

"I'd be okay with not being a dad." Cole threw his opinion in as he followed Shayla into the plane.

"I used to think I would, too." Grayson looked down at Lily's cherubic face. "But I might have to reevaluate that decision. If I ever reach that point in my life, that is."

When he cleared his throat and straightened, Shayla gave Lauren a pointed look. "Oh, is that so? I wonder what could have caused you to reconsider." She threw Lauren a wink.

Lauren turned hot and pink. "Lily is a pretty beautiful baby. She might even convince Cole if he isn't careful."

Shayla rolled her eyes. "Not unless she has magic powers."

"I'm pretty sure we have more important things to discuss right now." Cole pulled at his collar.

"Like what?" Shayla grinned.

"Like doing our job and keeping this baby safe." Cole gave her a stern, disapproving look.

Shayla shrugged, grin still intact.

Lauren excused herself to move aside and make the phone call.

Her mother was glad to hear from her and kept reassuring her that both she and Britlan were making it fine. She questioned Lauren about her whereabouts and why she was calling from the strange number, but accepted Lauren's proclamation that she wasn't able to tell her.

When Lauren returned, Grayson was asking Cole and Shayla if they had uncovered any more information on Savannah Reid's whereabouts.

"No." Cole shook his head. "Nothing significant. Every lead has turned up a dead end, according to Peter Finney. He's the one heading the search."

"She's staying one step ahead of them, which leads me to believe she has help from someone with lots of experience running from the law." Grayson tapped a finger on the armrest of his seat. "Or maybe we should take a closer look at Peter Finney and anyone he is closely associated with in the Marshals Service."

Lauren focused her attention out the window of the plane as it lifted into the air. She was pressed back against the seat and felt the sudden pressure, dip and swell in her middle as they left the earth behind.

She focused on Lily. On how Grayson had become so good with her over the span of just a few days.

Lauren must have drifted off with her thoughts, because the next thing she knew, Grayson was waking her to tell her they were landing.

"I'm sorry. Is Lily okay? Where are we?" She couldn't get all of her questions out fast enough.

"You're just fine. I'm sure you were exhausted. Lily's fine, too." He paused. "And we're in Texas. Near Austin."

"Isn't Texas where you thought Romine and Savannah were hiding out?" Lauren still felt fuzzy-headed from sleep. "Wouldn't we want to get Lily farther away from Romine rather than closer?"

"Well, we've kind of hatched a new plan." Grayson gave her an indulgent look. She didn't know what to make of it.

"While I was sleeping?"

He hesitated. "It's been in the works."

"But I thought there was another marshal in charge of finding Romine and Savannah. What other purpose could you have for coming to Texas?"

"There is. But eventually Romine is going to come after Lily himself, so we are going to put him on notice. If we can lure him in, we should easily end up cracking this whole case." He frowned and she felt like there was something he wasn't telling her.

"Wait. You're not thinking of using Lily as bait, are you?" Lauren still didn't quite know what was going on, but it was the only thing she could think of.

"Actually… Savannah and Romine aren't the only ones in Texas. Senator Reid is here. He's visiting an old friend who lives in Austin. We've been in contact with him."

The plane touched down, jolting them and interrupting Grayson's words. She looked at Shayla and Cole, who were both suspiciously quiet.

"He wants the baby." Lauren's soft words held a touch of anguish.

Grayson looked at Shayla. She nodded. "You should tell her everything."

Lauren crossed her arms at her chest. "Yes. You should."

Grayson sighed. "He wants to see her, just to assure himself she's safe. We don't think Romine will let that happen. We're going to leak word that Senator Reid is meeting with us. We think Romine will come after her himself."

"What? You *are* using Lily as bait! You can't do this, Grayson." Lauren was furious. How could he endanger Lily like this? And to think she had begun to believe he cared for them.

"It isn't like that, Lauren. She'll be safe the whole time. I guarantee it. The plan is to take Lily in another direction, but Romine doesn't have to know it." Grayson gave her a pleading look. "This is the only way to get this over with."

She felt the hot sting of tears behind her eyelids.

Shayla took Lily and followed Cole from the cabin of the plane, taking the nebulizer and diaper bag also. Lauren rose to follow them, but Grayson stopped her.

"Wait, Lauren. We need to talk about this. Let me explain."

"There's nothing to explain. It's just a case to you. It's all about getting the job done. I don't know what made me forget that."

She squeezed her eyes shut. This wasn't supposed to happen. She didn't want to care for Grayson or Lily, but she did. And now Grayson was going to know. And he was going to reject her.

Grayson's chest squeezed with emotion as he watched Lauren fight her tears. This was exactly why he had to wrap this up now. He wasn't supposed to feel this way about Lauren. The longer the case dragged on, the worse it was going to hurt when they parted ways. And no matter what happened with Lily, they would have to part ways eventually.

"It is a case, yes, Lauren. I have a job to do. I would never endanger you and Lily, though. We have a solid plan and I'll keep you and Lily safe. I hope that in less than twenty-four hours we will have Romine in custody, and you will be headed back to DC to return to your life."

He meant the words to be comforting, but he somehow didn't get the response he'd expected. Her face scrunched up in something like a wince, and she shook her head.

"How do you know Lily will be safe just because you capture Romine? Aren't there other people after her, too? Didn't we just determine that?" Lauren looked away from him.

"She'll still be under protection, probably most of her life, just because of who her grandfather is. And who her father is, of course. Ideally, though, we will soon put an end to both gangs' existence. That is the ultimate plan."

"But who will take care of her? How do you know her mother will come around? Do you trust Senator Reid to care for a baby?" She spewed the questions without waiting for a reply.

"Lauren, listen to yourself. You have to let that go. You aren't her mother. Her family has the right to decide who will take care of her, and it's up to them, not us. You're going to have to let her go eventually."

He hated to speak to her so bluntly, but she needed to start realizing it. Lily was someone else's child. Lauren seemed to have forgotten that.

However, the devastated expression she wore was more than he could take. He folded her into his arms, drawing her close against his chest. He breathed in her sweet scent and felt her shuddering breaths. Her fight for self-control was unhinging him.

He eased away from her just slightly, giving her a tender smile. "You're tough. You can do this."

She shook her head. "Why did you have to drag me into this, Grayson Thorpe? I'll never forgive you."

He frowned and laid a hand on her cheek. "I know. I'm sorry."

As he looked into her luminous eyes, something snapped within him, like a band that pulled him away from her, then released him to connect with her. She stared back at him. Had she felt it, too?

He didn't wait to find out. He leaned in close, their faces only inches apart. "I'm not sorry for this, though."

When he knew she read his intentions correctly and didn't protest, he bent his head to her, touching her lips with his, gently at first, but then with more intensity. It was worse than he had expected—the tenderness he had imagined he would feel when he finally kissed her. He had been thinking about it for far too long. He eased back slowly, trying to read her eyes as he did so. They looked as lost in wonder as he felt.

She still looked stunned, but he turned and walked away from her anyway.

Why had he given in to that need to kiss her? He shouldn't have done it. He had to put some distance between them while he still could.

TEN

Lauren was in shock.

Had Grayson really just kissed her? Here she was, just wanting to hate him for not caring more about her and Lily, and he had to go and kiss her so tenderly she thought she might evaporate and float away. This was getting far too complicated. He was gaining far too much control over her for her peace of mind. She wanted to be near him, to know him better. She hadn't been able to resist falling for him. It had to stop.

Maybe it was a good thing this case was about to be finished. As unappealing as the idea of going home was to her right now, it was probably for the best. She had to get out soon, because his kiss had made her realize something. It was undeniable, really.

She was falling for Grayson Thorpe.

Wasn't it bad enough she had grown attached to Lily? Now Grayson had an emotional hold on her. It was all too much.

She was still standing there with her fingers against her lips when Shayla stuck her head back into the cabin. "Everything okay?"

Lauren nodded, too enthusiastically. "Yeah. Yeah. Just fine." She sounded silly, too.

She grabbed the baby's bag and followed Shayla off the plane, but not before she noticed the marshal eyeing her. A flush crept up Lauren's neck. Did Shayla know what had just transpired? No, that was ridiculous. Grayson wouldn't kiss and tell.

The expression made her blush anew. Now she was just being goofy.

Grayson didn't speak to her the entire time they were driving to the new safe house. He didn't look at her, either. Was he having regrets? And if he was, were they for kissing her or for the plan they had concocted?

Either way, she felt no sympathy for him.

The new house was nestled in the hills in the outskirts of Austin. Lauren was surprised at the terrain, expecting Texas to look more like a desert with some tumbleweeds and red plateaus. When she said so, Shayla giggled.

"Texas is big. There're all kinds of different terrain, depending on where you go in the state. Lush pastures, scruffy deserts, hill country, cities, beaches… It's like a whole country of its own down here." Shayla flung her arms out, waving them as if to take in the grand landscape.

Lauren nodded, feeling a little sheltered. "I really would like to travel more."

"Why haven't you?" Grayson asked the question as they climbed into the waiting car.

She turned to look at him. "Oh, you know, the usual reasons. No time, family commitments, working for my career goals…"

"I'm sure your sister and mother both would love to take a trip or two when she's feeling up to it. There are some memories worth making." His expression was pretty blank, but she was warmed by the things he said. He hadn't forgotten what she had told him about her family, but he also tried to encourage her to make the most of it.

"You're right. Maybe I can look into that and plan something during my vacation time. It might be a while before I get any time off after this, though." She thought of how her supervisor was likely to respond to her continuing absence, not seeing the landscape as it passed by her window.

"You might be surprised. It wasn't your choice that Dr. Covington sent you along. And I'm sure she'll vouch for you, as well." Grayson navigated the road without looking in her direction this time.

It was only a short drive, and soon they were getting out at a house in a quiet neighborhood. Shayla had taken Lily again, and while Lauren knew she needed to distance herself from the baby, as well, a part of her wanted to spend every single second with Lily that she could.

"Grayson." She said his name softly, but it must have been unexpected, because he looked a little thunderstruck when she faced him. He just waited, though.

"What if this doesn't work?"

His brow furrowed. "What do you mean?"

Surely he had considered the possibility. "If Romine doesn't show up, are you still going to just send me home? Lily still needs someone to take care of her." Her voice wavered. She wasn't sure how to ask the questions that burned within her. Was this it? Was she really about to head home and never see Lily again? Was he just going to wave goodbye and never see her again, even after that kiss?

He didn't answer right away. When he did, there was a deep sigh first. She wasn't sure what to make of that, so she tried to focus on his words.

"I don't really know yet. We will have to decide that when the time comes." He didn't look at her. Rather, he tried to look everywhere but into her face. Did he know what she was really wondering?

Lauren didn't know what else to say, so she just ducked into the house.

"Lauren."

The sound of her name on his lips stopped her where she stood.

"I—I will figure something out. I need—"

"Grayson." Cole called his name from the hallway, interrupting whatever he was about to say.

"We will talk later, okay?" And then he was gone.

Lauren felt empty when he left. Shayla was changing Lily's diaper and talking to her in silly baby talk. She couldn't even fully enjoy the sweet moment for the ache filling her chest. She wasn't supposed to feel this way. She wasn't supposed to become attached.

"Do you wanna talk about it?" Shayla's voice penetrated the fog of thoughts clouding her mind.

"No. Yes. I don't know, honestly." Lauren sat almost robotically. "How am I going to let this sweet little one go?"

Shayla offered her a soft smile. "I know this is difficult, Lauren, and I'm sorry. It's the nature of our job as marshals, but it doesn't mean we like it. And maybe you'll see her again someday."

"What do you mean I might see her again someday?" Lauren tried not to let hope swell within her.

"I mean... I don't know. Maybe I shouldn't have said that. I just know that sometimes things work out differently than we expect. But, also, is it really just Lily you're worried about?"

Lauren couldn't keep the shock from her face. "Do you mean...?" She glanced down the short hallway of the cottage-style house to where Grayson had disappeared.

"Yes, I mean Grayson." Shayla blurted it out in a stage whisper. "I've seen the way you two look at each other."

"What, is it like how you and Cole look at each other?" Lauren meant the remark to be teasing, but Shayla stiffened.

"That isn't funny. I would never want to have a relationship with someone as straitlaced and serious as Cole."

"I'm sorry, Shayla. I—" Lauren didn't have a chance to finish because Cole walked into the room at that moment.

"No one with any sense would want to be in a relationship with anyone as flighty and irresponsible as you, either, Shayla. So save your insults." Cole looked angry but sounded calm.

Lauren felt the awkwardness of being in the wrong place at the wrong time.

Shayla stood there stoically for a moment, then just turned and strode over to hand Lily off to Lauren. Without a word, she walked out of the house and didn't look back.

Lauren couldn't get any words out, just stared at Cole, then at Lily, then back at Cole again.

"Well, don't look at me that way. I didn't mean it." Cole frowned at her.

"Why are you telling me? She's the one who

needs to hear that." Lauren actually grinned at him. She kind of knew how he felt. She couldn't quite say the right things to Grayson, either.

Grayson couldn't stop pacing.

He needed to find a way to keep Lauren around for a little while longer. No, what he needed to do was to send her home and end this. Then maybe he would get over his feelings for her. That was right. He could admit it. He had feelings for her. But that didn't mean he had to do anything about it. In fact, it probably meant quite the opposite. It meant he should protect her from him and his toxic emotions. After all, he couldn't even help his mother. Why would a woman as wonderful as Lauren want him in her life? Maybe she thought she did now, but eventually she would see what his mother had. The Thorpe men just weren't enough to give a woman a happy life.

He would have enough grace to keep her from having to tell him that someday.

He knew Cole and Shayla were fighting, and he knew Lily was fussy from the lingering fever, but he couldn't face Lauren and her questions. She might not have been able to get the words out, but he had read the questions in her eyes. Was this it for them? Did he ever want to see her again?

Of course he did, but he just couldn't. Couldn't she see that?

His chest ached at the realization that came to him in that moment. He couldn't stand the thought of never seeing her again. He wanted to kick himself for letting this happen, but he couldn't help it. He knew the truth.

He had fallen in love with Lauren.

How was a man supposed to tell a woman he loved that he was no good for her? That he would never be enough?

His ego wouldn't allow it. So he would just have to drive her away. He didn't want to, but he cared too much for her to let her believe a relationship might ever work.

He hid out until it was time to prepare for their rendezvous with Senator Reid. They planned to meet in a quiet park, where there wouldn't be a lot of other people milling around this late in the evening, just in case Romine's people decided to do something stupid again. There would be plenty of extra security present if Romine happened to make it to their meeting place unhindered.

But he expected Romine to act before then.

Since nothing they had done was secret so far, Grayson was sure the kidnappers would be ready for them. It was just a matter of putting the plan in motion.

The clock kept moving and he couldn't put it off any longer. He still had no idea how to help Lauren through this. She was strong enough, but if she broke down saying goodbye to Lily, he didn't know what he would do.

He stuck his head around the corner and saw her holding Lily and saying little noises at her. The baby cooed back and made little faces at Lauren, from toothless grins to round-mouthed Os with wide blue eyes watching Lauren's face. It was amazing how much Lily was already capable of. He had decided Lauren was probably right—if the baby had been premature, it wasn't by as much as the hospital thought.

Lauren smiled at Lily with dramatic head shakes and silly words, unaware that Grayson was watching. His heart clutched just watching them.

How was he supposed to do this? He might need more help than he'd thought.

She looked up and noticed him there, and her expression sobered.

"Lauren, I know I said we would talk. I have to meet Senator Reid in forty-five minutes." He hated the way she flinched at his words. He wasn't sure if it was because his tone sounded harsh or just because she hated what she knew was about to happen.

"I guess it isn't up to me." Lauren's voice turned businesslike. "I have all of her things together. I wrote out specific instructions about her medicine and treatments, and the phone number for the pediatrician who last saw her. I can answer any questions—"

"Shayla is taking her to a new safe house. Without you. As soon as it's safe to do so, I will be flying you home." When he interrupted her, he was met with stunned silence.

"I just think it's for the best. I'll have it look like Shayla is going with me, and Cole will stay here with you. Once it's safe—"

"How can you do this?"

He was shocked almost as much by her assertiveness as he was by her calm tone. "It isn't personal. I just think it's best for all of us. You can say your goodbyes to Lily here. And if things go wrong, Shayla is a trained law enforcement officer. She will know what to do."

Lauren just stared at him, not bothering to keep the hurt and anger from her face now.

"You'll be safer here. I expect Romine to try to intercept us before we get to Senator Reid."

"I see."

"Lauren, please try to understand."

"I do. I understand."

He didn't know how to react to her cool response. He had expected passion and fury, not this cold acceptance. He knew it meant she was hurt and so angry with him that she wouldn't even argue. He tried to make her.

"You aren't even going to fight me on this?

I thought you'd have your teeth bared and your dukes up at the idea of me separating you from Lily."

She turned her back to him. "It's like you said. She isn't mine. I have no choice but to let her go."

He strode over to her and turned her around to face him. Despite her even tone, tears streamed down her cheeks.

He spoke her name and tried to take her into his arms, but she pushed him away.

"I'm in no state to accept comfort from you, Marshal Thorpe. I can't talk to you about this. Just do your job." She turned her back again, and this time he left her alone.

"I'm truly sorry, Lauren."

She didn't answer, just stood there looking out the window while he and Shayla gathered all of Lily's things and loaded the baby, carrier and all, into the SUV. He considered trying again just before walking out, but her rigid stance proved to be insurmountable.

His throat closed up as he pulled the door shut behind him.

Lauren almost didn't last until he was out of sight before the flood of tears released. She couldn't remember when she had ever hurt so much. She couldn't even draw in a breath. It just made her chest seize with unbearable pain again.

She knew it was foolish. She had known all along that this was all just temporary. Her head knew, but her heart was stubborn. In her heart, she and Grayson and Lily were already a family. Somewhere along the way, she had allowed the fairy tale to become a reality.

And the fact that Grayson had left her behind this time made it so much worse. What if they lost the instructions for Lily's medications and breathing treatments? What if she got worse and Shayla waited too long to get her to the hospital? What if Senator Reid ended up with custody and she was raised, for the rest of her life, by hired people who didn't truly love her like Lauren did?

What if Lauren never got over loving her?

She could ask herself what-ifs all night long—there was nothing she could do about any of it. So she prayed. She prayed and cried.

When she finally dried her eyes, she went to find a glass of water.

She was surprised she hadn't seen or heard anything from Cole, but she supposed he was giving her some space, since he wasn't particularly fond of emotional displays of any kind.

The sky had grown dark and the only sounds were of evening insects trilling out their songs. Lauren felt alone and unsettled. She had to search a bit in the unfamiliar kitchen to find a glass. When she finally did, she took it to the fridge to fill it, and a shadow fell across the kitchen floor. A shiver crept up her spine, although she told herself it was probably just Cole. She was being silly.

But when she turned, the cold nose of a pistol met her at close range. She followed it up an arm to the icy eyes of the ruthless Arnie Romine himself.

She opened her mouth, but he shook his head ruefully. "Go ahead and scream. There's no one to hear."

When he gestured to the back patio just beyond the kitchen's back door, she saw Cole's prone form, still as a stone.

"Is he—? Is he—?" She couldn't get out the words. Her breathing was fast, and fear was drowning her.

Romine shrugged. "I doubt it. But he's out cold and we'll be long gone before he wakes. Now. You're going to get in my pretty little car and we're going to take a drive. If you behave yourself, I might let you live so I can use you to get my kid before the marshal and the senator do something stupid. See, your marshal thought he could outsmart me, but it didn't work."

"What do you mean?" Lauren wondered if she could buy enough time for Cole to wake up.

"I'll explain in the car. But for now, put your glass down so I can get these zip tics on your wrists."

Apparently not. "Is that really necessary? I'm not going to fight a dangerous man with a gun."

"Just think of it as a precaution. You seem like the sensible type." He gave a mirthless laugh.

All the fight had gone out of her when Grayson and Shayla had left with Lily. Now she was just tired. She held out her wrists. "I don't know what makes you think Grayson would give up the baby for me. It's his job to protect Lily, not me. And Senator Reid doesn't even know me. So, you see, I'm pretty useless as far as bargaining chips go."

He frowned. "You'd better hope you're wrong. If that's the case, I'll just kill you and the marshal."

Lauren didn't doubt his words for a second.

He wasn't exaggerating about the car, either. She stepped outside to see a shiny new sports car sitting in the driveway, albeit a good distance from the house. She shook her head.

"You've got to be kidding me." A rueful laugh escaped her lips. What kind of sick joke was this?

"What?" His gruff question sounded almost like a bark. "It's a McLaren GT. Isn't it sweet?"

"I'm being kidnapped in a McLaren? Ridiculous. I always thought it would be one of those beat-up white vans with no back windows."

If he thought her humor was odd, he didn't say so. "It's got white leather seats. Don't get anything on them."

"I'll do my best, but I'm a little clumsy in zip ties. No experience." Her rueful remark hit home this time and he frowned. Apparently, he was through with her jokes.

"Take extra care or I'll find some horrible ways to torture you before I dispose of you." He said it in a low, threatening voice.

Any further attempt at humor to keep herself sane was lost. Lauren shuddered, but didn't reply. The gravity of the situation hit her full-force. Cole was out cold. Grayson and Shayla had no idea Romine had taken her. He was a good three times her weight, so overpowering him was out of the question, even if she could get past the gun.

Her blood froze. She was at the mercy of one of the most wanted criminals in the country. This was worse than bad.

They were almost to the park chosen as a rendezvous point with Senator Reid, and unease snaked up Grayson's spine like an unwelcome guest. Why hadn't he encountered any trouble yet? Where were Romine's men? Things weren't going as he'd expected at all.

He tried Cole. He was unsettled but not exactly surprised when it went to voice mail. Maybe he just didn't make it to the phone in time. He decided to try a second time.

Voice mail again.

Something wasn't right.

He thought about calling Shayla. She should

have made it to the new safe house with Lily by now. Maybe she had heard from Cole and knew why he wasn't answering.

But he'd already made a snap decision. Pulling onto the nearest crossroad, he turned around before he could even confirm his suspicions.

He called Shayla to make sure.

"I'll try, too." She seemed as concerned as he was about not being able to reach Cole. He should have called one of them back, at least.

After a few minutes, Shayla called Grayson. "He still isn't answering."

"Call Senator Reid. I have to go back."

"What should I tell him?" Shayla sounded shaken.

"I don't know. Tell him we've had a change of plans. Or we'll meet him later. I don't really care. Just tell him something." Grayson's mind was full of too many other thoughts to worry about Senator Reid at the moment.

"He isn't going to be happy." Shayla didn't disagree, though.

"Aren't you at all worried about Lauren and Cole?" His voice had risen a notch.

Her voice jumped an octave. "Of course, but... you don't think..."

His lips pressed together, Grayson accelerated, passing a jacked-up truck in a no-passing zone. "I wouldn't put anything past Romine."

She disconnected.

A few minutes later, Grayson's phone rang again.

"I've dispatched local police to the house," Shayla said. "There can only be one reason Cole isn't calling back by now."

Grayson nodded, though he knew she couldn't see him. "You're right. I hate to think the worst, but the way things are looking, it makes sense. Why else hasn't Romine tried something by now?"

Shayla was silent on the line for a second before she said anything else. "Romine thinks he's outsmarting us. So what is he doing?" She paused briefly before asking another question. "What could he stand to gain?"

Grayson considered her words. "Not much. Unless he has acted and we just don't know it yet."

"You don't think he has one or both of them held hostage." Shayla's voice shook slightly.

"Yeah, I'm afraid so. At least Lauren, anyway. He stands more to gain that way. And I have no idea where he would take her. But I can't think of any other plan he might have."

At almost that second, Grayson's phone rang in another call. He asked Shayla to hold on and then studied the unfamiliar number before answering.

He was disappointed that it wasn't Romine. A female voice answered through the Bluetooth speaker system, but it wasn't Lauren's voice.

"Marshal Grayson Thorpe?" The woman sounded slightly out of breath.

"Yes. Who is this?" He had no patience for niceties right now.

"My name is Savannah Reid. I believe you have my baby. Her name is Lily."

ELEVEN

Grayson glanced at his SUV's display screen in surprise and saw a strange number displayed there. "Yes. I have Lily. Where are you?"

"That isn't important. But I do need you to listen carefully." Her smooth voice held a threatening edge. It wasn't at all what he'd expected from her.

"Go on." Grayson didn't offer her any room to hedge.

"Your lady friend is on her way to being locked in a safe place until you can get Lily to me. I wanted to take her with me, but you had to make things difficult, so now we are going to have to do this another way. But if my father gets his hands on my baby before I do, I promise your friend will pay."

Grayson felt his throat close and all the air left his lungs. It was Savannah. She was behind this.

He'd had an idea it might be her all along, but he hadn't wanted to believe it. For Lily's sake.

"What do you mean you wanted to take her

with you?" Grayson needed to keep her on the line. However she had gotten his number, he felt it had something to do with what she was talking about now.

"It was Peter's idea. He said if we faked my kidnapping, no one would suspect anything. He was right. No one knew it was me. But now we can't get the money from my father because we don't have the baby. Arnie said it would be easy to get her, but he lied." Savannah sounded as if she was discussing the latest gossip rather than the fate of her child.

"Peter? Do you mean Peter Finney, US marshal?"

"Yeah, that's the one. He was originally assigned to protect me. It wasn't difficult to sway him over to our side. He likes money. A lot." Savannah gave a little laugh.

He felt sick to his stomach but didn't say anything at first. He took a deep breath.

"What do you want me to do?" Grayson shook his head. He should have planned for this. Savannah wasn't just with Arnie Romine; she was spearheading the effort to get Lily and hold her for ransom from Senator Reid. She had been behind the attempted kidnappings the whole time.

"There is an address coming through your cell phone right now. It will take you to an old abandoned barn a long way out of town. Come alone with Lily. If you cooperate, you can have the woman back in one piece in exchange for Lily. If you try anything stupid, you'll all have more holes in you than those fools we sent to the airport."

"You sent all of them?"

"No, just half of them. They were supposed to just surround you and take the baby, but those idiots with the Harmon gang saw an opportunity to double-cross us. They thought if they could get Lily first, they would get a cut of the money. I should have known better than to trust Angelina. It serves them all right."

The coldness in her voice sent shivers through Grayson. How was he going to make her think he had Lily?

"I have the address." He didn't say anything for a moment. He didn't want her to know Shayla was on the other line. "I'm on my way."

"Good. Now, I know you don't actually have Lily with you at the moment. Finney knows all about your plan. So go get her from Marshal McKenzie and get to that address. You have twenty minutes before we start cutting." Her cold voice came through just before the harsh click that indicated she had disconnected.

Cutting?

The idea of Romine taking a blade to Lauren's smooth skin chilled his blood.

"That's not gonna happen." Grayson couldn't

even begin to let that image take hold. He was talking to himself but didn't care.

He reconnected with Shayla's call and explained the latest development and the new plan. She protested as soon as he said he was taking Lily alone, though.

"No. Absolutely not. You need backup."

"I can't take the risk. If I show up with another marshal, they could kill Lauren." Grayson couldn't take that risk.

"Not if they don't know I'm there. Hide me. Either you are picking me up or I will find you." She seemed to be taking this situation as a challenge. "This will work. They'll never know I'm there."

"Shouldn't you see about Cole?" Grayson still wasn't sure it would work.

"I think this is more important right now. While you were on the other line, I heard from headquarters. The police found Cole with a large goose egg on his head. Disoriented, but he will be fine. You need me more right now."

Shayla sounded more serious than he had ever heard her sound. He should still probably argue. But he knew she was right. He needed backup. Who knew what could go wrong with these situations?

"Okay, fine, you can go with me. But we have to get there fast." Grayson could just see her grinning in victory.

Only a couple of minutes later, he had Shayla and Lily and they were on the way to the address. She picked up his phone and checked out the GPS to see where he had to go. "Ugh."

"Am I gonna make it in time?" he asked, fully aware of what she was doing.

"It's going to be close. Are you sure we should take Lily?" Shayla eyed him.

"Have a little faith." He grinned.

"Oh, I'll be exercising my faith-praying." Shayla nodded at him.

"What is the GPS saying on the distance?"

She spouted their expected arrival time.

He had about twelve minutes left to get to the barn. And, according to his GPS, the destination was about eleven minutes away.

Lauren fought against the helpless feeling attempting to swallow her whole. The fear was trying to overwhelm her. The thought of Lily, though, renewed her strength.

Romine had taken her to an old, run-down abandoned farm and tied her up in the back of a tumbledown barn among dusty stacks of discarded farm equipment. Then he had left. She wasn't sure if he'd left completely, or if he had just left her alone in the barn. She never heard the McLaren start up, so she thought he was still outside somewhere.

Inside, however, her mind was racing. For one, she was glad she wasn't afraid of rats and spiders, because there was no doubt this place was full of them. Besides that, she had plenty to be afraid of without considering what might crawl all over her unhindered with her limbs bound.

She spent most of her time praying and asking God to protect Lily and Grayson. She also prayed that Grayson would just let Romine kill her and keep Lily safe, if that was the only way to protect the baby.

But she knew Grayson too well to believe he would do that. He might not care for her the way she cared for him, but he had too much honor to let anything happen to her. It was just one of the little things she loved about him.

The minutes stretched on and a noise outside caught her attention. Another car? No way could it be Grayson, so she suppressed the surge of hope that tried to well up. The sound of a slamming car door and arguing voices confirmed her suspicion. Whoever had just arrived was definitely not here to rescue her.

And who was she to just sit there and wait on a knight to come and rescue her, anyway? No, it had to be up to her. If she could find a way to escape, maybe Lily would be safe.

The zip ties held her wrists securely, but her feet were loosely bound. She wiggled them a bit and found the restraints loosened the more she kicked. If she could get her feet free, she could at least run. It would be tough with her hands bound, but not impossible.

While she kicked and worked at her bound ankles, she scanned the barn for the most likely means of escape. A window to her right was cracked open slightly and she decided the odds were good that she could somehow wedge it wide enough to slide through. She was looking for any tools she might use to help prod it open with her hands tied when a noise alerted her to someone coming in.

"Well, look at that. The little mouse is still right where you left her." Savannah Reid made the remark with a flip of her long golden hair.

Lauren couldn't have been more surprised when she saw Savannah walk in. She didn't much look like she had just had a baby. She didn't look very motherly, either, in her tight-fitting, expensive leather skirt and cashmere sweater. "Savannah? You're working with Romine? Shouldn't you be trying to protect Lily from him?" Then she shook her head. "Grayson was right."

"Working with him?" Savannah snorted. "He'd have been arrested and received the death penalty by now if not for me."

Lauren had no idea what these two had planned for her, but she knew the longer she could keep them talking, the better her chances of survival would be. "So you kept him from getting arrested? How did you do that?"

Savannah looked self-satisfied but didn't really answer. "I have my ways. You're certainly nosy."

"I guess so. But I thought he was in charge of the gang. Did you take over? I've always heard women have better leadership skills. And your friend Angelina? Is she with your gang?" Lauren tried to use Savannah's assumption to her advantage. If she thought she was just curious, maybe she would continue to talk.

"Angelina and Harmon work for us now, if you must know. Some of their people are still angry over things that have happened in the past and they're trying to break away and start their own... business. It's causing some friction, but we'll get them straightened out. Most of the rebels were killed at the airport, anyway. Unfortunately, though, so were some of our best people."

Lauren shivered to think of how cold her attitude was toward those causing tension between the two groups.

Romine just watched the two of them, expression bored, as Savannah sashayed back and forth in front of Lauren. Her expensive shoes were getting dusty, but she didn't seem to notice.

"And what about your father? He doesn't want to overlook your, um, boyfriend's criminal activities?" Lauren paused. "Or doesn't he know he's your boyfriend?"

Savannah sighed. "He cut me off when he first found out about Arnie. But I've been pretty convincing. He thinks I broke up with him when I supposedly just found out about Arnie's business dealings. That's why I planned to let him think someone else kidnapped Lily. But the hospital wanted to keep her since they thought she was premature, and Arnie was getting impatient to get out of the country. See, I gave a false due date. Lily isn't a preemie, just small. We were going to get ransom money from my father so we could leave. But your boyfriend showed up too soon and ruined the whole plan."

"So all you really wanted was money? Doesn't your gang have money?"

"Not enough, and it's tied up in the organization. Arnie's people would have something to say about us taking a huge chunk of the business's money to go on a permanent vacation, and he has to have help getting a hold on it. It was set up that way to protect him, but the plan backfired when he needed money to leave quickly. The marshals are ready to arrest him at any moment. As it is, we can't get out of the country for any reason, not even to travel. We would be arrested before we could ever board a plane, unless we can bribe my father's man to fly us out on a private jet. But we need lots of money to do that." Savannah gestured at Romine angrily. "I don't know why we can't just buy one." She mumbled this last statement. It seemed his wanted status was hampering her luxe lifestyle.

"Well, what about Lily? Do you plan to raise her somewhere else? In another country somewhere?"

Romine snorted. "Vannah's no mother. If she can't afford to hire a nanny, she's up a creek."

Savannah shot him a hateful look. "This was your idea. I didn't want to be a mother. You knew that. I should have never listened to you. I won't make that mistake again."

"I didn't see you coming up with a better plan," he practically growled. "So we'll just see about that, princess. You don't like getting your hands dirty."

"Shut up, Arnie. We have more important things to do than argue right now." Savannah glanced at Lauren and then looked down at the expensive watch on her wrist.

"Time's almost up."

"He'll be here." Savannah motioned toward Lauren as if that was somehow significant. Was she hinting that Lauren had something to do with Grayson's arrival with Lily?

Lauren had no idea what that was about. She was still worried about Lily, though. "So you plan to hire a nanny and take Lily with you out of the country?"

"Why? You wanna apply for the position?" Romine snickered.

Savannah ignored his comment. "Only if my father won't. He has more experience dealing with nannies than I do." Savannah's tone indicated this was a sore subject.

"Were you raised by a nanny, Savannah?" Lauren couldn't imagine what Savannah's life must have been like as a child. It would have been far different from her own.

"More like nann*ies*. I had a new one every year or two."

"I take it that wasn't a pleasant existence?" Lauren didn't have to fake the empathy in her tone.

"Most of them were just my father's girlfriends that he wanted to keep close. It was convenient." Her expression indicated the convenience wasn't for her.

"And where was your mother?" Lauren asked the question gently, fearing the answer.

Savannah shot her an angry look. "Traveling. Right up until she left. Now, do you need to know any more dirt from my past? Look it up on the internet."

Romine laughed. "Oh, they don't leave out the good stuff, either."

"Enough." Savannah snapped at Romine and he sobered.

"I'm sorry, Savannah. That must have been a tough childhood." Lauren meant the words, but the woman stiffened.

"I don't need your sympathy. I have everything I need."

"Except the baby," Romine chimed in before she could silence him with another look.

"That's about to be remedied. I think I hear them pulling up now." Savannah took a Tiffany-blue Glock from her waistband and moved to point it at Lauren. She gestured for Romine to go to the door.

"Don't screw this up."

Grayson pulled up to the barn, a McLaren GT and an Audi R8 sports car looking sorely out of place in the run-down surroundings. Where exactly did these two goons intend to put a car seat? And what was their plan? He had spent the last ten minutes trying to figure it out so he would be better prepared.

He got out of the SUV and moved to start getting Lily out when he heard the voice of his nemesis behind him. "Just put your hands up. I'll get the kid."

When Grayson did as he commanded, he turned to see Romine holding a gun pointed right at him.

He gripped it with one hand and quickly searched Grayson for a weapon. Grayson held his breath. He had been wise enough to discard his weapon, but he had stashed a small knife in his boot. It was uncomfortable but might come in handy for a lot of things.

He just hoped Shayla could stay hidden in the rear cargo compartment until they could gain the upper hand.

Romine decided against the wisdom of turning his back to Grayson to pull the car seat from the SUV and gestured for Grayson to retrieve it. Though he was a good-sized guy, Romine was softer than he was strong. He was a bit round in some places, and he didn't have the build of someone who spent a great deal of time on his physical fitness.

Lily set up a howl about the same time Grayson reached in for her, and Romine winced. "Do you not know how to shut up the kid?"

Grayson almost found it comical. "She's your kid."

"Aren't you a comedian." He jabbed his Ruger toward Grayson as if in warning. "Shut her up. I can't deal with a screaming kid."

"She probably needs a diaper change."

"Great. Well, hurry up, Mr. Mom. Just make her stop that screaming."

Grayson had to say changing a diaper with a

gun to his head was a new experience. He did it quickly and picked up Lily to cuddle her to his chest. He prayed silently as he did that God would intervene for the sake of this tiny girl. He did his best to comfort her with his gentle touch, and she calmed in his embrace.

"Aw. Ain't that sweet. Head to the barn." The sarcasm in Romine's voice grated on Grayson's nerves.

"So what's the plan?" Grayson moved cautiously so Romine wouldn't do anything stupid.

"We're going into the barn. I'll take the kid, and we'll tie you up with your girlfriend in there." Romine's voice had a nasty edge to it.

Grayson was relieved to see Lauren unharmed when he walked into the barn. They were at the mercy of these two criminals. His only consolation was that Shayla would get suspicious if he didn't return in a reasonable amount of time.

For a moment, panic washed over him. If anything went wrong and Lauren or Lily was hurt, he didn't know what he would do. He was human. Things could go wrong. He knew only God could guarantee their safety.

He uttered a quick, silent prayer for guidance and protection for them all.

All of the thoughts rushing to mind at the sight of Lauren had him questioning his resolve to remain alone for the rest of his life. His heart did something funny in his chest, and in his mind, he knew it was too late to temper his feelings. He was in love with her. The only question was what he was going to do about it.

Lauren looked worried yet relieved at the sight of him. But he wasn't sure what other emotion lay behind her eyes. Was she just attached to him because of his protection, or was there something more? Did she share his feelings, or was he just hopeful that she did?

One thing was sure—he had to get them out of this mess before any of it could even matter.

If he had ever wondered if Savannah was really so coldhearted, she proved it as she barely spared her baby a glance when Grayson brought her in. "Good. Now we can get the plan moving."

"Already on it." Romine took Lily from Grayson and set the baby, carrier and all, on the dirt floor of the barn, then secured Grayson to a post where a stall had once stood.

Grayson looked at Lauren, trying to silently communicate with her. They had to remain calm and wait for the right time, but they would make a move as soon as Lily was safe. And, unless he underestimated her, Shayla was already strategizing their rescue. She'd been hidden when he had left her, but she had a good plan in place, he was sure. But he couldn't let Romine suspect anything.

The phone call Romine placed wasn't what

Grayson had expected. Romine spoke to someone named Jonas and told him to bring the senator.

"Why are you bringing my father here? He isn't supposed to know I'm a part of this!"

"You don't think he knows by now? Besides, I've come up with a new plan. While he's getting my name cleared, he's gonna loan us his private jet so we can get out of here right away, just the way you wanted, baby."

"He isn't going to do that." Savannah glared at him. "That Cessna is his baby."

"Sure he is. I can be persuasive. Besides, he can come along. He won't want to miss our island wedding. Surprise." Romine looked inordinately pleased with himself.

"And what makes you think I want to get married like this?" Savannah's face reddened with fury. "I want a huge wedding with all the society people there."

"Like I said, I can be persuasive." Romine's tone had lost all joviality now. "Besides, how do you think that's going to happen when I'm a wanted criminal? And you probably will be, too, soon."

Lauren looked at Grayson, eyes wide. He knew exactly what she was thinking. These two were out of their minds.

While the couple argued, Lauren motioned with her eyes and wiggled her feet and legs. Her ankles were practically free. How had he not noticed?

And how had Romine and Savannah not noticed? He gave her a tiny grin before the two looked back in their direction.

Lily began to cough, sending Lauren into high alert. "Her breathing treatment… Savannah, you've got to give it to her. She has RSV. If she has a relapse, she could die."

Savannah looked irritated and only mildly concerned. "I don't know anything about all that." She waved around a freshly manicured hand, nails so long it brought Cruella De Vil to Grayson's mind.

"She has a serious respiratory virus. Her diaper bag has the equipment and medicine she needs inside. Please. I wrote down the instructions and put them in the bag, as well." Lauren was all but crying as she pleaded with Savannah.

"Is this some sort of ploy to get us to untie you so you can escape?" Savannah narrowed her bright blue eyes at her.

"No, I promise. If you look in her bag, you will find the prescription labels on the medicine. You can call the hospital and verify her diagnosis and the necessary treatment."

Savannah frowned. "Why would I want to go to all that trouble?"

"Because a baby's life is at stake here. Don't you care at all for the life of your child?" Lauren's face revealed her disbelief. It was as if a fragile bubble of hope had shattered around her.

"Of course. I went to a lot of trouble to have this kid. She does me no good if she's dead. My father wants her alive. It's like he thinks it's his second chance because he did such a poor job of raising me. He told me so when he found out I was pregnant." Savannah said the cold words so flippantly that Grayson winced. Even Romine looked a little shocked.

"If you don't want to untie me, I can talk you through it. Just please make sure Lily gets her treatment." Desperation edged Lauren's voice.

Savannah sighed. "I have a better idea. Why don't you just take care of the baby and I'll hold my gun on you just to make sure you don't do anything stupid. And in the meantime, Arnie can hurry up and get my father here with our money so we can go."

Her voice rose on the last statement, but Romine just raised an eyebrow at her. "You think I'm not ready to get out of here?"

Grayson took in the tension between the two. Their arguing could be a distraction he could use to his advantage. Neither would be at the top of their game with all the fussing between them. And if they got frustrated, one of two things would happen. Either they would be careless and make it easy for him and Lauren to take the baby and escape, or they would do something stupid and ruin their own plans. He planned to be prepared for either scenario.

The problem was that trying to retrieve the baby and rescue Lauren at the same time would be a bit tricky. Lauren had proved to be strong and resourceful, but this would be a new test for her. And it was a matter of life and death this time. He had faith she could do it, but it scared him to take the risk. So many things could go wrong. And he still wasn't sure why Savannah and Romine were keeping him and Lauren alive. He knew it would just be a matter of time before they killed them if they didn't get away. These two wouldn't want any witnesses to their crimes, especially not a US marshal. He prayed silently for an opportunity, as well as wisdom and protection for them both.

Romine was on the phone again, telling Jonas to hurry up. When he disconnected, he shot Savannah a disgruntled look. "Fifteen minutes."

Her response was a displeased groan. She finished untying Lauren's hands and kept her Glock trained on her while Lauren gave Lily her breathing treatment.

Lauren was doing her best to ignore the gun's threatening presence, but Grayson could see she was rattled. With good reason, too, since the volatile situation between Savannah and Romine made it even more likely Savannah would freak out and pull the trigger. Lauren's hands were steady, though, and her spine stiff and straight, sending a clear message that she would not be easily intimidated. She would not back down where Lily was concerned.

Grayson wanted nothing more in that moment than to take that burden from her slender shoulders. Time seemed to stop entirely even though he scrambled to come up with a plan.

A noise outside let them know as soon as Romine's men arrived with Senator Reid.

Romine went to the door, then thought better of it, looking suspiciously back at Grayson. He stood there in limbo for a moment, but one of his men came bursting through the door. Two more followed, carrying the trussed-up senator, whom they had rendered unconscious.

Behind them, in walked none other than US marshal Peter Finney.

Grayson growled when he smirked at him. "Filthy traitor."

His words were low, but Finney had no trouble hearing him. "This side pays better."

Grayson ignored him and his ridiculous wink. He was too busy taking in the rest of the scene. He didn't expect to have any trouble when it came to overtaking Finney, considering what he already knew about the man's mental and physical capabilities.

Grayson wasn't thrilled to see the numbers

increase. The presence of all of Romine's men would make it more difficult for them to escape. He began recalculating his plans.

"Daddy! Oh!" Savannah ran to her father, forgetting the Glock in her hand as she let it dangle in her grasp. "Arnie, how could you?"

"What? This wasn't planned. I mean…"

"Ugh! You are ridiculous!" Savannah knelt beside her father's limp form where the men had deposited him in the dirt.

"It was… I mean, I didn't… Savannah, I—" Romine looked thunderstruck.

"Just leave me alone."

Savannah turned into a different person in the face of her unconscious father. Grayson didn't know what to make of it. This went against every opinion he had formed about the woman so far. Was it sincere, or was she just a fantastic actress?

Romine ordered the men to keep a gun on Lauren and one on Grayson, but he was distracted himself, trying to pacify Savannah. He came down on one knee beside her, speaking in her ear so softly that Grayson couldn't make out his words.

Savannah pushed him away. "It wasn't supposed to happen like this. He wasn't supposed to get hurt. You said he wouldn't. Why did you do this?" Savannah's voice was almost a shriek.

"He's going to be fine, Vannah. I promise.

Please calm down." Romine didn't seem to know what to do with her in this state.

Grayson spared a look in Lauren's direction. Her face showed sympathy and confusion. He felt the same way. What was going on with Savannah Reid? And, more important, could they use it to their benefit somehow? Get the baby out of this dangerous situation? Lily was being unusually quiet.

Savannah had cradled her father's head in her lap, and he let out an occasional mumble. "Daddy! Daddy, can you hear me? It's me, Savannah."

She sounded like a little girl again and Grayson imagined she was feeling like she had wandered back into the past. What had happened between father and daughter? Was there more to this than Grayson knew about? Or was it just a game?

"I'm sorry, Daddy. I didn't mean for you to be hurt." She said the words in a way that made Grayson wonder if she was referring to today or sometime in the past.

"Savannah?" Her father's eyes opened. "What? Why are you here? I thought you'd been kidnapped. They abducted you, too?"

He was groggy, but his tone was indignant. "They won't get away with this."

Romine shot Savannah a look, one brow elevated, but she ignored him.

Grayson still wasn't sure if Savannah was sincere or just putting on a show. Was she trying to convince her father this wasn't her plan, or was she having a change of heart? What was she trying to accomplish? Her behavior didn't line up with her actions of a few minutes prior at all. The situation was becoming that much more dangerous.

Lauren watched Savannah carefully, suspicion that the woman was insincere filling her. Where had this sudden devoted love for her father come from when she couldn't lift a finger to help her own sick child? Savannah was up to something. Lauren held Lily closely.

Senator Reid, beginning to come around, looked at Savannah in confusion. "What's going on?"

"Arnie Romine has my baby. He's trying to get ransom money from you to get out of the country before he gets arrested. Daddy, what are we going to do?" Savannah turned on the tears.

If the senator noticed Savannah was free of any bindings and held a gun in her hand, he didn't seem to think it odd. He murmured words of consolation to her. "The baby… Savannah, where—?"

Lauren was anxious for an opportunity to get Lily to safety. Would this be a good time to get her out of here?

She glanced at Grayson, but he gave a tiny, almost imperceptible shake of his head. Had he read her thoughts?

In any case, it was a bad idea. Even if she could safely get Lily out of the barn, there would be other problems. First, how was she supposed to drive and hold Lily safely with no car seat if the SUV couldn't be used to get away, and how could she get out of the barn with the carrier and the baby before someone could stop her? Also, what if they killed Grayson in retaliation as soon as they found her gone? She wouldn't leave without him.

There was also the issue that she could be accused of kidnapping Lily, even though she was just trying to get her to safety.

So what should she do? Did he have a plan? It seemed like everyone's plans had been upended.

Lauren continued to pray and to wait. The drama between the Reids and Romine played out in front of her. Had Savannah been planning this all along? Were the rest of them playing into her hands? Lauren had a number of suspicions where Savannah Reid was concerned. Thanks to her instincts, none of them was good.

Her attention was drawn back to the scene at hand, though, when Senator Reid began to protest. "No, Savannah. I won't leave without you and the baby."

She grasped his hand. "It's okay, Daddy. I have it all figured out." She winked at him, and then, before the senator knew what was happening, one of the men jabbed a needle into his arm, rendering him unconscious once again.

Lauren gave Grayson a surprised look. They didn't have much longer to act.

Savannah opened her mouth, confirming Lauren's suspicions. "First thing we should do is take care of Marshal Thorpe and little Nurse Mommy here." She kept her gun on Romine but nodded her head toward Lauren. "I see the little mouse is too scared to even try to escape when her hands are untied."

Savannah's disdain inflamed Lauren's temper, but she resolved to stay composed. "I wouldn't do anything to endanger Lily." She kept her voice quiet, calm and collected. She wouldn't give Savannah the satisfaction of seeing her upset.

"Oh, isn't that sweet." Savannah's voice, however, was grating and full of sarcasm. "Kirk, take the baby away from her and tie her back up."

The smallest of Savannah's minions, though still a good two-hundred-fifty pounds of brawn, reached for the baby, but Lauren backed away. He grunted and kept advancing on her. The thought of this brute taking Lily made her more than a little furious.

He lunged at her and she kicked hard, striking him in the shin. He howled in pain, enraging Savannah.

"Bull!" She bellowed the word. "Kirk could use some help with the mouse."

Had she called the other man Bull? Lauren had no time to ponder the question further, for all thoughts fled when he pulled a Ruger and aimed it at her face.

"Hand over the kid," Bull said, his tone menacing, though his expression was childlike.

Lauren tilted her head to one side and slowly began to ease her grip on Lily. Something about this man was different.

"Bull? Is that your name?" Lauren asked the question quietly, close, where the others couldn't really hear.

"Nah. Name's Lucian. But Miss Reid don't like it. Says it ain't a mean name."

Lauren glanced at Lily. "I like Lucian much better than Bull," she whispered as she reluctantly let Kirk have the baby.

Lucian didn't lower the gun, but something changed in his expression. Lauren put her hands in the air.

"Untie my father." Savannah's expression was smug. She lifted her head and gave her blond mane a toss.

"Should I tie this'n up first?" Lucian gestured at Lauren.

"Just kill her. We have no more use for her." Savannah didn't even blink. She might as well have been commenting on the weather.

Cold fear swept through Lauren, the gun in Lucian's hand already aimed at her, meaning she didn't even have seconds to spare.

Grayson was still gagged and bound, but she could hear him struggling against his restraints just behind her. He made a tremendous amount of noise.

Lucian cocked the gun. His brow furrowed.

"Hurry up!" Savannah insisted.

As he was about to squeeze the trigger, the door to the barn burst open. Lucian pulled the nose of the gun toward the ceiling as it fired.

"Nobody move! US Marshals Service. We have you surrounded." As Cole shouted the words, splinters of wood rained down on Lauren's head. She looked at Lucian, openmouthed, and he actually grinned and winked at her.

Lily was wailing and Shayla swept in to take her from Kirk's beefy grasp, aiming her Glock at his thick head until he complied. Finney tried to run. Another marshal wasted no time in taking him down.

Cole quickly cut Grayson loose, and a swarm of other marshals converged on the criminals.

Romine, however, grew desperate before anyone could snag him. He thought he saw his chance and he took it. He kicked the gun out of the nearest marshal's hand, causing it to go off in the process. Romine fled while everyone hit the floor, snatching Lauren and putting a knife to her throat as he backed out the door of the barn.

"Come after me and she dies." He didn't have to say the words. Lauren already knew what he intended.

She started to go limp in his arms, but as her muscles went lax, he dug the knife viciously into her neck, so she changed her mind. She could feel the warm stickiness of her own blood trickling down her neck.

"Don't be stupid." Romine spoke close to her ear. "I've had enough of stupid women today. But she got what she deserved."

At his words, Lauren looked around the barn for Savannah and realized she lay on the ground, unmoving. The bullet from the marshal's gun must have struck her somehow.

Lauren gasped. "Is she dead?"

"Who knows? Might have just grazed her. Hope she is, though." He proceeded to call Savannah a long list of grossly unpleasant names as he dragged Lauren out of the barn.

Grayson was watching, his expression tormented. She feared she might never see him again.

I'm so sorry. I love you. She mouthed the words just before the barn door slammed between them.

TWELVE

Grayson had no trouble reading Lauren's lips--or her mind. He was a little disappointed in her, frankly. She thought he was just going to let her go? That she would never see him again? Ridiculous. Didn't she know him by now?

He ran for the barn door as soon as Romine had disappeared out of sight with Lauren. He leaned around the door frame cautiously to see what was happening before ducking low to follow on out the door. He made it to the R8 undetected. The marshals outside had guns aimed in Romine's direction, but with Lauren being held hostage, there wasn't much anyone could do to stop him. He'd held Lauren in front of him until he was inside the car, dragging her in over top of him. The snipers couldn't get a clear shot for more than a split second.

Fortunately, Romine hadn't noticed Grayson squatting behind the Audi R8. He had been too busy dragging Lauren into the driver's seat. Holding his gun on her, he forced her to put the car in Drive and hightail it out of the yard. Grayson's sympathy for her made his stomach tighten. She was probably physically ill at this moment. He felt pretty ill on her behalf. All he could think of was her words to him as Romine dragged her away. She loved him? Did she mean it?

Savannah had left the keys in her Audi, just as he'd suspected. He waved Cole into the passenger seat and started the engine. Keeping an eye on Romine's direction, he took up the chase, his mind full of questions. Was Romine just using Lauren to facilitate his getaway, or did he have another plan? Did that plan involve Lily? Would the baby's future continually be vulnerable if Romine got away?

The McLaren flew around a curve in the road at breakneck speed and Grayson tried to maintain the pace as he followed. He was a little impressed at Lauren's driving skills, even though he knew Romine was giving her orders from the passenger seat.

They were headed farther out of the city, so Grayson tried to think like a criminal. Where would Romine go? Where would he need to be to feel like he had a chance at escape?

"He has to be headed to meet up with some of his gang members. There's safety in numbers. We can't let him get that far," Grayson declared, gripping the wheel, his expression determined.

"What can we do to stop him?" Cole looked around dubiously. There was a lake on one side of the road and, across a steady line of traffic, trees on the other. The McLaren surged ahead, forcing Grayson to have to focus to keep up. The GT sped around cars as the lanes widened once more.

Cole had his Glock in his hand. "Should I try to shoot out the tires?"

"Too much risk in all this traffic. And it could cause Lauren to wreck. We don't want to put her in that kind of danger." Grayson zipped around an SUV crossover that had moved into his lane. "We need to get some backup. If he gets to a gang of his people, we're finished."

"Maybe that doesn't have to happen." Cole pulled out his phone.

"What are you going to do?" Grayson, determined to catch up with the McLaren, wasn't even sure what he was going to do when he did. He knew Romine wouldn't shoot Lauren while she was driving, but if Grayson forced him to a stop, what then? Could he shoot Romine and risk hitting Lauren?

"What if we could negotiate with Romine? I mean…that's why he wanted the baby, right? To have some way to negotiate?" Cole was texting someone. "I'll see if I can get his cell number."

Grayson closed in on the McLaren. "I'm not sure. He might be too desperate at this point—" A car cut him off, interrupting his thoughts. "Cole, try to keep eyes on them. I've lost them in this traffic."

"I still see them right now. Moving straight ahead." Cole leaned this way and that, trying to get a better view.

"I'm doing my best to get around it, but it's almost like the driver of that car acted on purpose. He cut me off and then slowed enough that I can't get around him." Grayson frowned and gripped the Audi's gearshift in frustration.

"It's annoying enough when you have nowhere to be. It makes me wish we had lights and sirens in a situation like this." Cole strained forward, trying for a better sight line. "I think they've turned."

"Uh-oh. Do you know where?" Grayson hadn't seen the McLaren turn off, and there was more than one intersection ahead.

"I'm not positive, but I'm trying to watch. I think it's about three turns ahead on the right." Cole eyed every turn they approached, straining to catch a glimpse of the dark blue McLaren.

"There!" Cole pointed at the next turnoff and Grayson braked hard to make the exit.

Too many curves and hills stretched ahead of them. Grayson's abdomen tightened. It would be tough enough to gain on them. Keeping eyes on them wouldn't be easy, either. "Of course he took her on the most difficult route possible."

He tried to focus, but all he could think about was Lauren. About her last words to him. About how much he wanted to tell her he loved her, too. In fact, when he had her back, he wasn't going to waste any more time. He needed her in his life. For the rest of his life.

While he was thinking about marrying Lauren, though, Romine was trying hard to take her farther away. The road led through a residential area, causing Grayson to have to reduce his speed far more than he would have liked.

"Watch it!" Cole shouted as a bicycle pulled out of a nearby road just slightly ahead of them.

Grayson braked and swerved over, but in the process lost sight of the McLaren. "Where are they?"

Cole stretched and leaned but came up with nothing. "I don't know. I don't think they turned."

Grayson bit back his frustration. He kept following the road but didn't catch sight of the sports car for far too long. "What now?"

"I'm pulling up GPS. Let's see if we can get an idea where this leads or where they might have gone." Cole studied his phone while Grayson drove and kept his eyes peeled for the McLaren. It was like they'd disappeared.

"Anything?" Grayson was at a loss for where

to look. The hills surrounding Austin seemed like enemies.

"The road goes through to another highway after several miles. But there are also a lot of obscure turnoffs. I have no idea where most of them lead. Some are just residential areas, but a few go on through to major highways. They could have taken any of them." Cole sounded almost as frustrated as Grayson felt.

"Call the sheriff's department and have them issue a BOLO on the McLaren." He waited until Cole had the dispatcher on the line and gave him the tag number. He'd memorized it in the brief moments they'd been close enough, just trying to keep his mind on something other than what Romine might do to Lauren if things went wrong.

"I'm about to take a risk here—" Grayson didn't give Cole time to disconnect the call he had just finished up "—and stop me if I'm wrong. But if you were Romine, would you take any chances you didn't have to take?"

"No… What are you thinking?"

"I'm thinking the first chance he gets, he's going to either let her go or kill her." Grayson could barely force the words out.

"That doesn't sound promising. So, if we've lost them, how do we keep that from happening?"

"We're just going to have to find them before he has the opportunity." Grayson's jaw flexed.

He couldn't consider anything happening to Lauren. He couldn't stand the thought. She had told him she loved him, but he had been too shocked at the time to do the same. He had to let her know. He had to have a chance to make a life with her.

"So what exactly are you going to do?" Cole prompted, interrupting his musings.

"Find them and beat them to the cutoff. Hold on." Grayson jerked the wheel and cut through a residential area under construction. The houses were still just skeletons of wood frames, the road not yet paved. Still, Grayson pushed the Audi as hard as he dared.

"Keep GPS pulled up, but if my instincts are on point, we should come out ahead of them just before they reach the highway." Grayson stayed focused on the road.

"I don't think this road is even on GPS yet." Cole was frowning at his screen.

"That's okay. Just make sure we continue to make progress toward the main highway. Everything else is irrelevant." Grayson's focus never wavered.

Cole reached for anything available to hold on to as Grayson accelerated, fishtailing a little on the loose gravel on the dusty road. The Audi recovered and Grayson was grateful for the expensive sports car's handling.

He noticed Cole looked a little green. "Are you okay?"

Cole's tense bearing came to mind, and Grayson thought of how Shayla always accused him of being uptight. He realized in an instant what the problem was. "You have an unsteady stomach, don't you?"

"I get a little…um, sick sometimes." It sounded like it pained Cole to admit it. "I know. I try to hide it from Shayla, but it's something I can't help."

Grayson felt a little guilty. "Oh, man, I'm sorry. No, I mean—that's… It's perfectly normal to get a little motion sickness."

"Not in our profession." Cole muttered the words.

Grayson eased off the accelerator a bit. "Is that why you always give Shayla so much trouble over her driving? You don't feel sick if you drive."

Cole just nodded.

At the same time, a flash of blue appeared on a hill in the distance.

"Grayson, look!" Cole pointed and Grayson followed Cole's finger to see the McLaren appear again in the distance. "You were right. But you're going to have to hurry."

A glance at Cole confirmed he was down for the adventure, despite his nausea. Grayson floored it, letting the dirt and gravel fly. The Audi responded to the punch of the pedal with an enthusiastic lurch, and Grayson's adrenaline surged in response.

The tires bounced and danced as they flew over the gravel road, but the Audi admirably handled the moves. They advanced on the intersection in what seemed far slower than the high rate of speed Grayson read on the dash.

The McLaren also advanced on the intersection at a high rate of speed but had to slow to make a couple of curves, giving Grayson just a slight advantage. He used every last bit of courage he had, flying into the intersection and spinning to a stop just as the McLaren topped a small rise, barely in time for Lauren to brake.

She did, but something went wrong. The McLaren slowed but didn't completely stop. The impact jarred the Audi fiercely and Grayson realized too late that Cole was going to take the worst of it.

When the jolt of the impact had subsided, Grayson spoke. "I'm sorry, buddy. Are you okay?" He tried to examine Cole from his place behind the wheel, but Cole waved him off with a grunt.

"Be…fine. Go. Get your girl." Cole threw his head back and closed his eyes.

His reminder refocused Grayson on Lauren, and he looked up in time to see Romine force her out of the car. She stumbled and he shoved a gun at her again.

Fury surged through Grayson. "Romine, stop!" He'd yelled the command, but his nemesis just stared him down.

"Don't look like you're in much of a position to give the orders here." Romine gripped the gun with both hands for emphasis.

"What are you going to do? Run on foot? With a hostage? We have backup on the way. Might as well give it up. We can make a deal." Grayson kept his voice even, but he wanted to rush Romine in a rage. Lauren's terrified expression was inflicting a lot of damage on him.

"I got backup on the way myself. Not gonna work." Romine gave him a smirk. He urged Lauren to start walking with the nose of his gun. The desperate, panicked look she wore was almost more than Grayson could handle. He needed to make a move—now.

"Romine, come on. Let her go. Haven't you had enough of this yet? Be a man. Escape on your own two feet. Don't drag her down with you." Grayson knew it was a gamble, but maybe in light of what had just happened with Savannah, it might get through to him. Grayson sent up a silent prayer.

Romine stumbled but held fast. "Not gonna happen. Sometimes brains are more important than brawn."

Grayson took that as his answer to pursue this path of reasoning. "Is that what Savannah taught you? She certainly didn't use brawn to take over your organization."

Romine was shaking now. "She didn't take over the organization. You don't know what you're talking about. We had a plan."

"Well, don't take this the wrong way, but it looks like she is the one in charge. If she's still alive, that is." Grayson took a cautious step toward them.

Lauren, eyes wide, was listening intently. She seemed to be waiting for her chance. He prayed she wouldn't do anything that would endanger her life.

"I don't know why you think you know anything about it. Savannah's been dodging her protective detail for years. And she's too tough to be down long. I'm sure she's fine. Besides, I have the money. I don't need her anymore. Whatever you think you know is wrong." Romine puffed up like a junior-high bully trying to assert his dominance.

"Oh, I'm sure that's true. But the scene we just witnessed back there speaks volumes. I think I can fill in the blanks." Grayson didn't feel nearly as relaxed as he was letting on. He had to get Lauren away from the man before he did something that might hurt her.

"Ha! Yeah, you don't know the half of it. We can still make it work." He threw up his hands in a wild gesture. "She might seem like she's not stable, but she makes it work. Her daddy never suspected. She should have been an actress."

Lauren took the opportunity. While the gun was disengaged, she dropped her body like a limp doll, causing Romine to lose his balance. She then swung a leg around like a martial artist, knocking the gun from his hand. It discharged, and while Romine tried to recover, Grayson dived at him, pushing Lauren out of the way.

The two men rolled around on the ground, wrestling for dominance. Grayson worked to focus on his adversary, though he saw Lauren out of the corner of his eye. She was going for the gun.

Romine must have also noticed; he released Grayson and lunged for Lauren. Grayson grappled for him, swinging one leg out in a fierce kick to throw him off balance. Romine stumbled, but regained his footing, reaching for Lauren again. He managed to grab her arm, but she kicked the gun out of his reach. He released her to go after it and she fell back hard.

About that time, a shot rang out.

Romine's right hand, which had been reaching for the gun, was suddenly hanging limply at his side. He howled in pain and shock. He wouldn't be so easily defeated, though, and reached for her with his other hand. This time he was too slow. Grayson tackled him, rolled him over and cuffed him before Romine could get another surge of strength.

Wondering where the shot had come from now that it was over, Grayson swiveled his head around to locate the source of the gunshot.

Cole stood, unstable on one leg, several yards away. He gave Grayson a wink and a salute before collapsing into a heap.

"Cole!" Lauren yelled, seeing him collapse a few yards away. "Grayson, what happened to him?"

Grayson had already leaped to his feet and was running toward him, leaving the cuffed criminal facedown and protesting in the middle of the road. "The McLaren hit us on his side. I don't know how badly he's injured. Call for an ambulance." He tossed her his cell phone as he ran.

She caught the cell phone in surprise and did as he asked, but as she got closer, she could clearly see that Cole's leg was broken at the femur. Knowing the thighbone to be the strongest in the human body, she feared the severity of his other injuries. It was amazing no one else had been hurt from that impact. Cole had, unfortunately, taken the brunt of the force alone.

Lauren crouched beside Grayson. "I should call Shayla. That leg looks bad."

Grayson appeared startled at her words. "Yeah.

Is there anything you can do for him until the ambulance arrives?"

She tried to smile. "I'll do anything I can." She bent over Cole and began to examine his leg. "I don't know how long it will take them to get here, but I can probably have it splinted by then."

"I'll call Shayla. You take care of Cole."

Shayla almost beat the ambulance to them. She got out of the SUV as paramedics were checking Cole.

"Lily is in the car seat, safe and sound." She tossed the words to Lauren as she collapsed beside Cole opposite the EMT bent over him. "What have you done?"

Lauren bit back a chuckle at Shayla's words, but then ran for the baby. Having Lily safely in her arms again was the sweetest balm for her recent trauma. She breathed deeply of Lily's scent as she cuddled her close.

"That was one of the bravest things I've ever seen." Grayson's words behind her poured over her like warm water, making her tingle from head to toe.

"I'm sure it looked kind of risky to you. But I was desperate." She turned to look into his face, seeing so much emotion there her throat began to close.

"You couldn't wait for me to save you?" There

was a hint of amusement in his tone as he stepped a little closer.

She smiled. "How did you plan to do that?"

"I wasn't sure. But I would have figured out something. I had to." He put a hand on her cheek.

She tilted her head to one side. "Is that so?"

He nodded. "I'm going to kiss you now, if that's okay?"

"Yeah, it is. But—"

"We'll talk later." His lips met hers, gently at first and then with the intensity of a man staking his claim. A little sigh escaped her. Lily lay silent in the shelter of their shared embrace. Lauren's only regret was that she couldn't put her arms around Grayson in return.

He pulled back. "Don't ever scare me like that again."

She laughed. "I'll do my best, but no promises."

"Speaking of promises—"

"Marshal Thorpe?" A man in a police uniform interrupted his words. "I need to speak to you about the arrest."

He nodded at the man and looked back to her. "I guess it will be later." He winked at Lauren before turning to follow the man.

Lauren watched him go, wondering about what he'd wanted to say to her. She hoped it wasn't what she feared.

Now that they had Romine in custody, Grayson

wouldn't need her anymore. Air refused to enter her lungs at the idea of his telling her goodbye.

She wandered over to a tree and sat beneath it. Suddenly, the idea of waiting around to hear Grayson tell her goodbye was more than she could bear. She couldn't do it.

What was she going to do? He had left her sitting alone and she couldn't bear it. Her thoughts were consumed with Grayson, though, and all the things she had never told him.

Like how she wanted to spend the rest of her life with him.

The tears started and wouldn't stop. How could she ever expect someone like Grayson to return her love?

She couldn't. And the idea that she was about to have to let Lily go was also almost more than she could bear.

Lauren put her head down and let the tears flow. Maybe it was the anticlimax of being in a hostage situation and nearly being killed that made it so bad. At least, that was what she told herself. But it was more about losing Grayson and Lily. She knew that, even if she didn't want to admit it.

Suddenly, Grayson was kneeling in front of her. "Lauren, are you okay?"

She sniffled. "I'm fine. It's just—everything. It's too much." She gestured around her, but his expression said he wasn't buying it.

"What's really going on, Lauren? You've been crying. Have you changed your mind? Wish you hadn't mouthed those words to me back at the barn?" He ran a gentle finger along her cheek, trying to tease a smile out of her. But it wasn't working.

She couldn't stand it. "I'm not ready to tell you goodbye. I love you."

She'd blurted the words out so quickly that Grayson sat back in shock. Then he laughed.

"Well, don't laugh. It isn't funny." She was a little angry that he thought her emotions were so unimportant.

"It *is* funny, because I have no intention of letting you tell me goodbye. I love you, too. I can't stand the idea of letting you go."

"But you said we needed to talk about some things. You said—"

He put a finger on her lips. "We do need to talk about some things. I was going to ask you to marry me. I just couldn't get an opportunity."

"To…marry you? But before, you said—"

"I know what I said. But I don't want to live without you."

"Really?" Her eyes filled once more.

"Really. So let me do this right." He pulled her to her feet and then got down on one knee. He took her hands in his. "Lauren Beck, would you please do me the honor of becoming my wife?"

She pulled one hand away to put over her mouth. "Yes! Oh, yes! I would love to be your wife, Grayson Thorpe."

He kissed her then. A long, slow and sweet kiss. When she looked up, her eyes were clouded once more.

"Oh, Grayson, what about Lily?"

He grinned. "I have something to tell you about Lily." He kissed her fingers. "Something I think you'll be happy to hear."

"Well, what? Just tell me."

"It seems Senator Reid has decided it would be in Lily's best interest to be in WITSEC. Before we set up the meeting, he opened up to me a little bit. I didn't want to mention it until I knew how things would go. But… He doesn't want to give up his own high-profile life, but he thinks it would be best if Lily Reid disappeared." Grayson smiled.

"But how does that work? Who will be her legal guardian?" Lauren didn't know what that meant for Lily's future.

"She'll be adopted under another identity," Grayson explained.

"Oh. Well…good for Lily. I pray she gets a loving home and parents that truly adore her."

"Oh, she will. I believe, since I am already a marshal and would stand a good chance of having her under my protection anyway, that they might allow us to adopt her."

"What? Oh, Grayson! But will the senator know?"

"It will be secret. I'm sure he will have a good idea, but he wouldn't ever jeopardize her safety by telling anyone. It might take a little while, though. Paperwork and all that."

"He's sure he wants to give her up?"

"We had a long talk. He thinks it's in her best interests to be raised elsewhere, in light of the situation. He's realized it might be better for her to be raised by two loving parents."

"That's generous of him. It couldn't have been an easy decision for him to give up his grandchild." Lauren looked away, blinking furiously with emotion.

"There were a few things he noticed that helped convince him. I might have elaborated on a few of them." Grayson grinned at her.

"Like how much I adore Lily? You're so amazing." Lauren kissed him again.

"You're pretty amazing yourself, Lauren Beck."

Her heart was overflowing as she settled into his perfect embrace.

EPILOGUE

Today was the second-happiest day of Lauren's life.

They were bringing their baby girl home to stay as their official daughter, and though it was a tight race, this day fell slightly behind the day she had married Grayson Thorpe as the happiest.

To protect her identity, Grayson and Lauren had decided to name her Riley Elizabeth Thorpe, and though the new name had taken some getting used to, it seemed to fit the happy little girl perfectly.

Everyone was waiting at their home when they arrived with Riley. Lauren's mother, sister, all of Grayson's brothers and, of course, Shayla and Cole.

Britlan, having immediately fallen in love with Riley, had received news of a transplant shortly after meeting her. She had undergone surgery and was recovering well, now focusing on becoming Riley's favorite aunt. Lauren's mother, Donna, couldn't have been more excited about her new granddaughter and had brought in frilly pink dresses galore for her.

Grayson's tough brothers, also eager to make fools of themselves over the tiny critter, talked to her in silly voices and argued over which one of them she liked more.

Grayson had recently resigned from the US Marshals Service but had received a prestigious job offer as an adviser for White House security. They had both decided the new job would be in Riley's best interest—if anyone ever came looking for her because they would be expecting her to be under the protection of a marshal.

Lauren kept her job in the NICU at Grace Memorial, but contrary to her fears of not being eligible for promotion, she'd been offered a position as a nursing supervisor and happily changed to daytime hours. Things were working out better than she had hoped.

Savannah Reid had recovered from her gunshot wound only to be tried and convicted alongside Arnold Romine and several of his gang members. She would spend life in prison. Her father hadn't even tried to lighten her sentence. US marshal Peter Finney had suffered the same fate, to say nothing of his humiliation for being labeled a traitor.

Grayson's mission had been a complete success.

"Congratulations!" Shayla hugged her and

oohed over how much Riley had grown since she'd seen her last. Cole grinned as he shook Grayson's hand and patted him on the back. They talked quietly for a few minutes, giving Shayla a chance to hold the chubby Riley, who was now an active, squirmy little thing.

"We don't want to encroach on your happy day, but we have something to tell you." Shayla smiled broadly.

"Not at all. Please do tell," Lauren urged, glancing at her husband with a hopeful smile.

"Well, Cole and I are getting married." Shayla beamed as she held up her ring for all to see.

"Wow! Congratulations, you two!" Lauren hugged Shayla again and winked at Cole. "I knew you'd come around."

Grayson echoed her congratulatory remarks. "Looks like it's going to have to be Little *Mrs.* Sunshine soon."

"Ha ha. Very funny, Grayson." Shayla laughed even as Cole turned pink.

"There is someone I'd like you both to meet before you leave." Grayson was all seriousness now.

A pretty woman in her midfifties stepped out from behind him, and Lauren clasped her hand as Grayson made the introductions.

"This is my mother, Lena."

Lauren and Lena greeted each other with shy hellos, and after Lauren finally reached in with a hug, the woman smiled, beginning to show some signs of feeling more at ease.

At Lauren's urging, Grayson had reached out to his mother after finally locating her. Now a widow, Lena had been afraid of rejection from him and his brothers after leaving and not coming back. But once she had explained the whole story, they had eventually forgiven her.

When Lena had been released from prison, for stealing prescription painkillers, the boys' father had refused to let her see them. Even though she had gone through extensive rehab, he had gone so far as to obtain a court order against her. Sadly, he had never forgiven her before he'd died, and she had been afraid her sons wouldn't, either.

The Thorpe men were still trying to work out their relationship with their mother, but it was at least improving.

Riley, however, had won them all over instantly and was currently thriving as the center of attention.

As Lena took the baby into the living room to encourage all of the guests to have cake, Grayson leaned in to give Lauren a kiss.

"Have I told you lately how happy I am that you are my wife?"

"Not since this morning, so please feel free to tell me again." She leaned into him.

Shayla poked at them both. "Come on, you two.

Plenty of time for that later. Right now, there's a new baby girl to celebrate."

Cole lifted his glass. "To Riley Elizabeth Thorpe and her happy family."

The guests echoed his sentiment. "To Riley Elizabeth Thorpe."

Lauren looked at Riley and then back at Grayson, thinking she couldn't be happier. As she looked around at their precious extended family, there was only one thought on her mind.

They were going to have a wonderful life.

* * * * *

If you enjoyed Attempted Abduction,
*pick up this other thrilling story
by Sommer Smith:*

Under Suspicion

*Available now from
Love Inspired Suspense!*

*Find more great reads at
www.LoveInspired.com.*

Dear Reader,

Thank you for joining Lauren and Grayson on their journey to protect Lily. They just happened to find love along the way. Isn't it great how God does that for us sometimes? I wanted to see Lily find the happy family she deserved. Lauren had a deep need to protect the innocent child, and while Grayson was initially leery of the newborn, Lily found her way into his heart. I believe taking care of newborns in the NICU, as Lauren did, would be a rewarding job. Though Grayson had a job to do, he had to use quick thinking to complete the task. He feared his own efforts would not be enough. It was only later that he discovered how much he needed to turn it over to God.

I hope you enjoyed the story. My email is ssmith.kgc3@gmail.com, and I love hearing from readers!

Blessings,
Sommer Smith

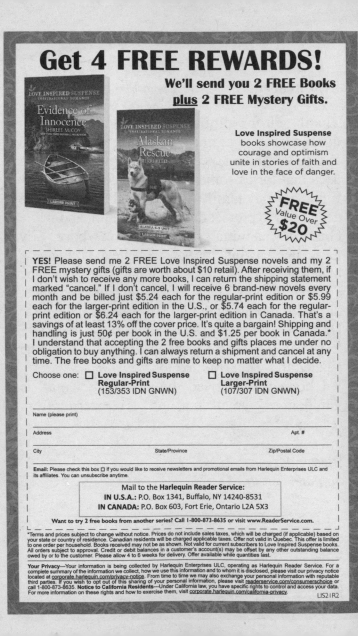

Get 4 FREE REWARDS!

We'll send you 2 FREE Books plus 2 FREE Mystery Gifts.

Love Inspired Suspense books showcase how courage and optimism unite in stories of faith and love in the face of danger.

FREE Value Over **$20**

Get 4 FREE REWARDS!

We'll send you 2 FREE Books plus 2 FREE Mystery Gifts.

Harlequin Heartwarming Larger-Print books will connect you to uplifting stories where the bonds of friendship, family and community unite.

FREE Value Over **$20**

HARLEQUIN SELECTS COLLECTION

19 FREE BOOKS IN ALL!

From Robyn Carr to RaeAnne Thayne to Linda Lael Miller and Sherryl Woods we promise (actually, GUARANTEE!) each author in the Harlequin Selects collection has seen their name on the *New York Times* or *USA TODAY* bestseller lists!

ARCTIC WITNESS
Alaska K-9 Unit • by Heather Woodhaven
When his ex-wife goes missing in the Alaskan wilderness after
discovering a body, Alaska State Trooper Sean West and his K-9 partner,
Grace, rescue her from a kidnapper. Now the murderer is on their trail,
and it's up to Sean to protect Ivy and the little boy she plans to adopt.

MOUNTAIN FUGITIVE
by Lynette Eason
Out on a horseback ride, Dr. Kathrine Gilroy stumbles into the middle
of a shoot-out. Now with US Marshal Dominic O'Ryan injured and
under her care, she's determined to help him find the fugitive who
killed his partner...before they both end up dead.

COVERT AMISH INVESTIGATION
Amish Country Justice • by Dana R. Lynn
Police officer Kate Bontrager never planned to return to her Amish
roots, but with a woman missing from witness protection in Kate's
former community, she has no choice. The moment she arrives for her
undercover assignment, she becomes a target...and working with her
ex, Abram Burkholder, is her only hope of staying alive.

HIGH STAKES ESCAPE
Mount Shasta Secrets • by Elizabeth Goddard
Someone is killing off deputy US Marshal Ben Bradley's witnesses
one by one, and he won't let Chasey Cook become the next victim.
But on the run with a leak in the Marshals Service and murderers
drawing closer, he and Chasey have no one to trust. Can he shield
her from danger on his own?

KIDNAP THREAT
by Anne Galbraith
A mole in the police department thrusts a witness's mother right into
a deadly gang's crosshairs. They'll kill anyone to keep Alice Benoit's
son from testifying. Now it's up to officer Ben Parsons to protect Alice
for twenty-four hours in a busy city...or a killer could go free.

SNOWSTORM SABOTAGE
by Kerry Johnson
After single mom Everly Raven finds her friend murdered inside a
chalet on her family's ski resort, the blame falls on her. With a blizzard
closing in and the killer's henchmen chasing her down a mountain,
Everly must work with FBI agent Isaac Rhodes—the father of her
secret child—to clear her name.
